HELL'S
WAITING ROOM

First Printing, 2021
ISBN 978-0-578-98054-6 (Print)
ISBN 978-0-578-98055-3 (eBook)
Blockhead
Block Island, RI

HELL'S WAITING ROOM

MAL STEVENS

Blockhead

Prologue

Hell has a waiting room. It's bigger than you would think. Or at least it seems to hold more people than you think it could. There is a line that snakes back and forth, forth and back, in those little corrals like amusement parks and slaughterhouses have; and all the timekeeping signs, the ones proclaiming "This many minutes from This point," are wrong. It's always much, much longer than what the sign says.

And eventually you learn that the line is just to get to a window with a DMV type bureaucrat who gives you a form in Chinese. Unless you're Chinese, then the form is in German. Unless you are a Chinese guy who speaks German, in which case the form is in Braille. Unless you're blind, then they tell you you've been in the wrong line this whole time and the line you need to be in is across the street and there are no crosswalks. They provide you a service dog, but it's a bad-tempered Chihuahua, also blind.

So, there's really no point to the line. Once you figure

that out, you move over to the green chairs to wait until you are called. The green chairs are plastic, the kind that are all attached together in one long bench of individualized green discomfort, and the bench is attached to the wall. Or bolted to the floor, for the unlucky souls in the middle rows. Slick green plastic you can slide off of if you fall asleep.

But you can't fall asleep because the televisions are so damn loud. All on different channels, fading in and out with the antenna's snow. Each channel is a different type of Telemundo, in Spanish with Latin subtitles, always Latin subtitles. So the Catholics can feel superior. They don't know what it says either but at least they know it's Latin. The crackle of the snow when the channels fade out is almost soothing.

Each green seat has a few cracks in it, as if it is a really, really old seat, but they come from the Hell Furniture Factory that way. So that if you sit the wrong way or wiggle too much, the crack will pinch you. Unfortunately, when you arrive in the waiting room it turns out that everyone is wearing super-short Lederhosen, so there is plenty of bare leg skin to pinch.

There are extremely smelly metal ashtrays like they used to put on plane seats. Way too small to accommodate all the butts you're about to smoke. Because they let you smoke, but only menthols. Unless you like menthols, in which case you have to chew tobacco and there are no spittoons. You have to use the little smelly metal ashtray to spit in, which is inconvenient for the rest of us.

Your best bet is to fashion your own ashtray out of a beer can, because you can't just ash on the floor. You have manners, after all. And there are plenty of beer cans around, since they let you drink beer. Nonalcoholic of course. Naturally, there's always some asshole who has turned a floater into an ashtray, and then knocked it over at some point.

Periodically, the door at the end of the hall opens and the Nurse, the scantily clad, almost sexy Nurse sticks her head out and whistles her little tune. She is almost hot, except she only has one eye in the center of her forehead, and you can tell she really enjoys calling the wretched souls down for their torture sessions. She sticks her head out and whistles her little tune, which is entirely too cheery for the circumstances, and on verse 4, she finally calls a name, all low and sultry, at which point a tiny Oompa Loompa sized demon in a Chef's hat pokes his head around the side of her waist and yells "Bam! Now we're cookin!" at which point a hot and stinky breeze blows through the place, just in case you were wondering if Hell was really hot.

It is, and it smells.

It gets fucking old really fucking fast. Bam. You start planning what you'll do when they call your name, specifically how hard you're going to punch that little demon chef when you get up there. But it's never your name, or really anyone around you on the green chairs, and never anyone who is in the line.

Unless you make a friend while you're there. Then they are the next name the Nurse calls.

And you get so bored, and so agitated from 37 TV's blaring different versions of Spanish TV with Latin subtitles, and sort of hungry, and you start wishing they would call your name. That the Nurse would stick her ugly little head out, whistle her little fucking tune and call your name. So you could get on with the eternity of torture, the wailing and the gnashing of teeth. You start praying for hellfire and damnation, anything to get out of this seat-pinching, obnoxiously foreign-languaged, crowded, smoke-filled waiting room with no windows. And that fucking whistle, over and over again, and never your name.

"Please, take me, you devil in a Nurse dress, bring me to the torturers! Let's get this party started!" someone will yell out.

If you hear it once, you hear it a thousand times down there. But of course, that probably only makes it take longer.

Once you get the hang of the Waiting Room, it really isn't that bad. You get used to menthols pretty quick, and those lederhosen are very breezy and freeing. Mmmm-mmm, leather.

You learn to function in this environment, this place that kind of sucks, but is definitely better than what comes next, better than what awaits you on the other side of the door. You don't really like where you're at, but you find ways to make it bearable.

A sort of tense comradery develops on the green chairs, and eventually you're all glad you are still there together. Every time a name is called, you breathe a little sigh of relief that it isn't your name. We all feign bravado, but really, who the fuck wants to be tortured?

At least out here in the Waiting Room we can smoke.

And we all begin to realize, that if we are stuck here, let's enjoy our time together as much as we can. And in that sort of hopeless situation people start to accept each other more, start to set aside their prejudices and animosities. There is no escaping here. And we all have to use the ashtray for one thing or another.

Strange confessional sorts of conversations begin to happen. No one really thinks it will sway the Nurse in any way, and it definitely will not help you with that little chef. But we all slip into this sort of carefree acceptance of each other and our strange habits and proclivities. People really seem to open up in the Waiting Room.

Pot helps. They let you smoke it, but it's definitely a low-quality bud.

For Wade,

who sometimes still dances

to the

Sky Lizard's Anthem

Contents

Contents ~ xiii

One

Katie and the Lizard

We moved into Hell's Waiting Room at the turn of the century. We didn't really know that's what it would become. It was unassuming, of course.

It was sunny the day we came to view the apartment, which helped the overall ascetic of the building. It was a giant, three story heap of a shit-pile, with crumbling brick and rotted windows. This was of course based on the windows that were still exposed. It seemed that at least a couple of apartments on each floor were boarded up, no window in sight.

The entire thing looked as if it would fall right over, if not for the prostitute leaned against it, holding the whole thing up. Between her and the newly replaced wooden staircase and decking, the deteriorating brick façade looked to be fairly well supported.

The daytime hooker watched us pull up in our beat down jitney, loudly announcing our lack of disposable income with every screech and clang of the beast as it shuddered to a stop and sputtered a few times as the engine died. Looking disappointed, but not surprised, she took a giant swig out of her Strawberry-kiwi Snapple, swallowed it, then blew an enormous snot rocket and sauntered around the corner.

The landlord, who was leaned against his freshly scrubbed Monte Carlo pretending the hooker wasn't there, nodded toward the grand wooden staircase in the center of the building. It led to the second-floor deck, which extended across the front of the whole building. There were smaller staircases at each end of this deck, leading up to the third-floor decking, which also ran the length of the building. Altogether, it was a massive structure of pressure treated pine that was in stark contrast to the deteriorating building to which it was attached.

I figured the city had probably raised a stink about the stairs and forced this massive staircase renovation. It was a bit like polishing just the tip of a terd, though, so I didn't hold out much hope for the inside of the building.

The apartment in question was at the top of the stairs with 2 neighboring apartments on each side of it. Two of the apartments on the bottom floor were boarded up, and one on the second floor looked boarded up. Between the boarded-up windows and the daytime hooker, the place did not give off the best impression.

"We'll take it," Randy said, first thing, looking up the stairs.

The landlord, who had turned toward the stairs as we disembarked from the car, looked back at us.

"Really? Without seeing the inside?"

"Ohhhh, what the hell? Let's take a gander, shall we boys. Jacko lead the way," Boyd said, grinning at the landlord.

And with that I hopped up the stairs two at time, with Randy quickly behind me.

Boyd smiled again at the landlord and pointed up the stairs.

"After you," he said, politely.

Randy and I were leaning on either side of the door by the time the landlord made it up the stairs. Randy stared at the landlord intently while I fished a cigarette out of my shirt pocket.

The landlord looked suspiciously at Randy as he worked the key into the lock. Randy was watching him intently, from inside the landlord's personal space, as if it was the first time he had ever seen a deadbolt operated in such a fashion. His eyes were wide and he made a little click sound with his tongue and teeth every time the landlord nervously glanced his way.

"Young man, I'm armed," the landlord said firmly.

"And I'd appreciate you to stop staring at me," he continued.

Randy grinned that big shit-eating grin he had, the one where his eyes softened and you could tell he really liked you and was just playing. He kept his feet in place but leaned way back and to the side so that his torso and head were far removed from the landlord.

He played a weird way, I always thought, but I always went along when he started a "freak out the new guy" game. I nodded and grinned at the landlord when he looked at me in bewilderment, wondering if I was going to try to make sense of Randy's game.

Boyd always said the problem was that Randy's judgement on who we should play with was a little off. I thought Randy's judgement in general was a little off.

The landlord, who was clearly someone who did not appreciate our games, threw open the door to the apartment with a distasteful shake of his head. He headed in and we followed him down a long hallway with both bedrooms situated across from each other. The bedroom doors were open to reveal identical square rooms with a closet and a window opening out onto the deck.

The hallway terminated by opening into the living room. There were no windows in the living room. The small bathroom and the kitchen were off the left side. A single light bulb hung from the fixture in the middle of the ceiling, its bright incandescent glow almost blinding after the long dark hallway.

"We'll take it," Randy said again.

Boyd and I nodded and the landlord ran back to the car to get the paperwork.

We spent the afternoon moving the couch from Boyd's mother's house up the stairs. More accurately, Boyd and I moved the couch up the stairs, because Randy was tripping out and drawing on the wall.

When we finally got it up the stairs, Randy was wrapping up his project. It was a Colt 1911 model .45, in black, life size, held by a muscular, floating arm drawn in red. We moved the couch over to the wall opposite the hallway, where you could sit on it and see down the hallway to the exterior door. Randy had drawn the gun on the wall across from us.

"Check this out," Boyd said, as he unscrewed the single bulb from the overhead fixture, and replaced it with a red bulb. He turned out the lamp Randy had stolen from his brother's room at home, and we were plunged into eerie red darkness.

More importantly, the red arm disappeared,

leaving only the pistol, which seemed to be pointing directly at us.

Randy was ecstatic. He flipped the lamp on and off a few dozen times, making the arm disappear and then reappear, disappear and then reappear. He declared that he absolutely refused to help bring anything else in until he finished the house warming gift.

Never ones to underestimate the importance of the artist's timeframe and methods, we told him to carry on, and went to get some beer.

When Boyd and I got back, Randy had all the lights out but the red one. It takes a minute to get used to the light, but your eyes do adjust, like being in a darkroom. Coming down the hall, we could see that Randy had hung a humongous tapestry of Da Vinci's Last supper on the wall behind the couch.

"Come sit down, come sit down," he said.

We sat down, on the couch, as it was the only furniture in the room. As we sat there, in only the red light, Randy explained where the other furniture should go, once we gathered it up and got it here.

Some of it sounded like stuff we had, my love

seat from my mother's basement would go against the wall across from us, under the .45 he had drawn on the wall. The chair from his dad's garage would go in the corner, next to the stereo equipment and the TV from Boyd's grandmother.

He said we would need a coffee table for the center of the room and some stools for the other corner. Boyd and I nodded along with him. We knew when he got an idea into his head it was best to just let him get it out.

"And the best part is the lighting, this red light is perfect because it relaxes them, and makes them feel comfortable and accessible," he concluded.

Before I could ask what comfortable and accessible really meant, and who "they" were, he continued,

"And the absolute most awesome part, is they can't see who is holding the gun!"

And with that he threw the switch for the floor lamp, bathing the room in light and revealing the Sky Lizard, who was the one holding the gun.

The Sky Lizard looked about how you would expect: a lizard face with big sharp teeth and beady little leering eyes. Eyes that seemed to watch every move you made, as he kept his gun trained on you. His tongue protruded from his weird grinning mouth, perhaps laughing at the fact that he had tiny little wings on his back that probably would not have been able to lift him off the ground, were he subjected to the laws of physics.

But you could see in his eyes that the Sky Lizard obeyed no laws, of physics, fashion, or otherwise. He wore a Hawaiian shirt and pleated slacks, but no shoes, on account of his claws. His tail trailed behind him, protruding from a cutout that must have been in the back of his pants.

Pretty unassuming, really, except for the gun.

And the fact that he was a lizard that could fly, a Sky Lizard. Boyd promptly wrote an anthem on bass guitar for him, which he would quietly play in the background when guests really started to open up about their lives. They mostly didn't know about the lizard, at least not at first. If they came around enough, they would see him. The Sky Lizard was there for our benefit anyway, not the guests'.

Catchy tune, though.

Randy would turn the light on and talk to the lizard when no one was around.

We worked hard to develop a space where

guests were not very comfortable, but not completely miserable either. We just wanted them to accept the limitations of the situation. A space where inhibitions could be loosened up, since you sort of felt like this was near the end anyway. You don't really like the environment, in the abstract, but you are sort of drawn to it; sort of drawn to the idea of making the most of a shitty situation, given the impending doom that awaits all of us when the Nurse calls our name. We are stuck here together, so let's make the most of it.

We outfitted our apartment with the best furniture and accessories we could find, trying very hard to stick to Randy's original interior design plan. Boyd was an excellent scrounger, could really find most anything you would ever need. We added another couch and the love seat for the living room, which constituted the Waiting Room proper. This also served as Boyd's bedroom.

He played it off like he was suffering, by not having his own room like Randy and I had, but really, the Waiting Room was the place to be. The couches were both a little gamey, but the one near the lizard was most likely to reach up and scratch you with a sharp spring or something.

We advised against lederhosen, even on the loveseat.

We had a broken-down coffee table, perpetually covered in garbage. The center piece was a stolen offering plate that we used for a communal ashtray, although we didn't let tobacco chewers spit in it. We did not have that menthol rule, so we did not have too many backer chewers anyway.

You could, of course, make your own ashtray out of a beer can, because there were plenty of those around.

We didn't have cable, or really any movies besides Cheech and Chong and Goodfellas, so mostly the TV was just on snow, at low volume, so as not to interfere with the music.

Randy hung up a shark's jaw he had on the Last Supper tapestry, with the teeth and gaping jaws around Jesus's head like a halo. He put a High Voltage sticker over Jesus's face.

Randy handled most of the artistic decorating, of course.

Randy hung some of his other weird art around. There was an oil painting he had done, this crazy worm looking thing that was coming out of a house and trying to eat you. And he had some paintings of some other vine looking shit; he was big on vines.

I wanted to help with the decorating, so one day I drew some cartoons on the wall behind the TV. A Smurf in a loin cloth chopping down the Tree of Knowledge of Good and Evil. I was not sure I knew what I meant for that shit to mean. Katie didn't know either.

"What the fuck is that supposed to be?" she had asked, scaring the fuck out of me. I had forgotten she was there while I was drawing, and it was one of the few times I ever heard her talk. Katie was almost mute most of the time. I had shrugged and drawn a giant dildo crushing the sun, which I figured would need no explanation to my semi-vocal art critic.

Katie was a teenage prostitute who stayed with us for a little while. We didn't really know she was a prostitute. We didn't meet her in that context. She was an acquaintance of somebody, but I can't remember who she initially showed up with. In any case, she just started coming over, and then started crashing there most nights.

It never occurred to any of us that she would probably have paid us in trade for a place to stay, so we never asked her for any sexual favors. Or maybe that's exactly why she was there, precisely because we never expected anything from her. We didn't really expect anything out of most people. Most people being useless shits that they are.

Katie would bring pot over, that I now suspect she turned tricks for, but that never occurred to any of us at the time. Everybody else brought pot over all the time too, and I never thought any of them were hookers. They were just people with pot.

Katie really liked Randy, a lot, but he was obsessed with this girl he had been on one date with.

"And besides," he told us one night, "Katie's too young."

He was about to graduate from high school and she was probably a sophomore if she had been in school. They keep these consent ages pretty low in some of these states, so it probably wouldn't really have been a problem, but we knew what Randy meant. He was taking graduation and shit really seriously, and was thinking about being a grown up and wasn't interested in a high school girl.

Also, he was obsessed with the other girl he went on a failed date with one time. She was off in college now, although I doubt she willingly provided that information to Randy. Thank God they didn't have the internet back then, and stalkers had to really stalk in person.

Katie was not in school, and I didn't actually go to class that second semester of college, so Katie hung out around the waiting room with me most mornings while the boys were in school. We didn't talk much, just hung out. Katie never talked anyway, and I generally only talk as much as the other person wants to.

So Katie and I spent most mornings like this: smoke a bowl, pop a Xanax, smoke some cigarettes, drink some coffee and watch some Cheech and Chong. She slept mostly, and would leave around noon and come back in the evenings with some pot.

We found out much later that her brother had been her pimp from when she was 10 or so. I suspect she was between pimps when she came to us, because it was not her pimp who came looking for her.

It was her mother, looking for her runaway daughter. Of course, it could have been mommy dearest all along who ran the hooking operation.

But she seemed genuinely upset about her daughter running off. Appropriately distraught as a mother, not as an employer. They talked it out and Katie pretty well moved in with us after that. We figured if her mother thought it was ok, who are we to argue with the matriarch?

And besides, people were always stopping over and crashing on one of the couches in the Waiting Room. Or the floor, or anywhere they could find a spot. It wasn't very comfortable, and not necessarily pleasant, but I think people felt like it was better to be in there with us waiting, than to be out there grinding in the world.

We existed in a drug induced haze, with poor lighting and bad music played through crackling speakers, enjoyed on uncomfortable seating. Yet we were always full, and the place would hold more people than you would think.

And we got all kinds.

Two

Margot

Margot, the debutante, loved us. Margot was hot. Margot was rich. Margot was going places in life. Her father was a dentist, and it was rumored that he had been in on the Bluegrass Conspiracy. We didn't know much about that particular conspiracy; Margot was about as close as we ever got. Apparently in the mid 80's, a man had parachuted to his death in a residential area with hundreds of pounds of cocaine and thousands of dollars strapped to his body. It was rumored he was a rogue DEA agent, or a former narcotics officer, or perhaps not even the person he was officially identified as. No one knew because the DEA and FBI swooped in and scooped up the body and that was the end of the official investigation.

Rumors swirled around this incident for decades. Was he just a mark, killed in the air and pushed out of the plane for some purpose? Was he a drug smuggler trying to rip off the South American cartels? Was he shot down by the FBI? Did he work for the DEA? Was he a rat, killed in such dramatic fashion to send a message? What became of the money and drugs he had on him? Or the money and drugs that must have remained in the plane, reportedly found crashed in North Carolina?

The story we heard about Margot's dad, from the son of his former partner in the dental practice, is that Margot's dad was a drug smuggler who used his private plane to fly out of Lexington and make runs down south to get cocaine, and then used the dental practice to wash the money. Our friend's dad found out about it and left the practice.

Or so the story goes. We did not learn all this from Margot, we did not realize her dad and the guy from the stories could've been the same guy. The story was that they had killed the DEA agent because he double crossed them, the dentist and his silent partner, the pawn shop king of Kentucky. But it was all rumors and inuendo. And we didn't realize we were that close to it until it was too late.

We met Margot at the bowling alley, while Randy was trying to hit on her. Boyd knew she was too smart and I knew I was too fucked up. Margot knew she was not fooling around with Randy, but she did want some of whatever I was obviously on.

Being a true dopehead, I was not about to share any of my portion of the oxys we were on with this girl. At some point in the junky's lifeline, dope becomes so much more vital than pussy. But it turned out she really only wanted to smoke some pot, so we told her where we lived and she agreed to stop by.

She drove her birthday present car over, dragging her friend along who was not feeling the vibe at all. She had looked dubiously at us as Margot informed her that we were all headed to our place to party. The friend harrumphed at Margot, or maybe it was at us, but she had climbed into Margot's car just the same.

As soon as she walked in, you knew Margot was hooked on the Waiting Room. She really dug it, one of those seemingly groundbreaking moments you have as a teen, when you realize some people get high right in their own living room.

"Holy shit, this changes everything! No more hiding behind the garage, and sneaking around. I am now a free human!"

Margot became a regular in the Waiting Room. She brought pot over all the time to smoke. Randy always harbored some resentment that she had shot him down that first night, so Margot was always bringing different friends with her to try to set him up with. Boyd would always say,

"Here comes Margot, bearing gifts of women and pot!"

To which Margot would curtsy, and introduce her femmes du jour.

We, of course, counseled Randy on staying away from minors, because Margot sometimes brought some very young girls around, eager to get high with their older friend Margot. He always left them alone and stuck to playing the music, which was always the best place for Randy to be.

Boyd and I left the young ones alone too. He always said older women knew what they wanted. And they wanted some kinky shit. And he was there for it.

Boyd had a steady thing going with our dope dealer; he claimed we were pimping him out for drugs, but he liked it, the fucking crybaby. What 19-year-old doesn't want to get high and fuck an experienced woman in her sexual prime? And leave with a bag of dope?

And she wasn't bad looking either.

I think he played up this whole victim angle so Randy and I would not get mad at him that he was getting laid and we weren't. I always got high, whether Boyd got laid or not, and that was what was most important to me.

I had a couple of girls I fooled with here and there, and that was all my drug deflated libido could handle anyway. And Randy... well Randy always wanted to get laid. But he was so fucking hung up on this other girl, and so fucking sad about his mom's suicide, and a little bit crazy on top of it. So, he pretty much operated on a dry cod at all times too.

Margot would bring her ritzy friends with her, slumming it over to the Waiting Room, where they were mostly left alone, because sexually exploiting teeny boppers is something that happens on the Nurse's side of the door. But we didn't tell Margot this, we just let her keep bringing her tribute of pot and booty, and we would smoke the pot and hang out.

Does it count as contributing to the delinquency of a minor if it's their pot? Probably, if it's your house.

But, there were always people over there, each contributing to their own delinquency. We were merely the custodians of the place. Randy handled the music, and mostly he did okay. You had to keep him out of the goddam Nielsen Smielsen, but generally he did alright.

This was during the old days, when a DJ had to change the actual cd to get a different song. And yes, you purists, he had some vinyl in the collection as well. He kept it spinning, all kinds of stuff from old 70's acid rock to 90's grunge and everything in between. He made one hell of a DJ.

It was good to keep him occupied with the music so he didn't talk to the guests too much. He would get frustrated, invariably realizing that tonight was not to be the night to get his peter wet, and he would start being a bit of an asshole. So, keeping him occupied with music was for the common good.

Boyd handled the concierge duties, tour guide of the trip, captain of the sinking ship, curator of Hell's Waiting Room. He was really in his element, adeptly steering conversations to places the occupants didn't know they wanted to go. Places you could tell they really needed to get to. He kept them comfortable and relaxed, coaxing their most interior thoughts and feelings out of them.

It was very therapeutic for some of them. They would come in to pass some time while they waited on the hell that was to be the rest of their life. They were casually planning to smoke a joint or two, maybe do some pills or something, and then go on about their business. But the Waiting Room would get to them, and they would end up discussing how they felt about their father, how they felt about their God, how they felt about their future and their relationships. It was fucking weird, but we just went with it. The Waiting Room has a mind of its own, after all, and within the metaphysical constraints to which it is subject, it acts as its own agent most of the time.

In short, to paraphrase Ted, the time traveling sage of our lives: strange things are definitely afoot in Hell's Waiting Room.

Three

Bubbles and Ed

The Waiting Room would bring together odd groupings of people, each stopping in on their own trip, but combining, mixing, swirling, and fading into the room's trip. We had future debutantes. We had hookers. We had two-bit dealers like Bubbles and his lackey.

The lackey's name was Ed, and Ed had a rough time. Ed was kidnapped and assaulted on his 16th birthday, trying to thumb a ride to his own birthday party. When he finally arrived, after the rapist van dropped him off, he was robustly ridiculed by everyone in the holler for not fighting off the rapist. Predictably, he descended into a dark place.

Fueled solely by drugs and alcohol, Ed looked like walking death. With Ed, you knew it was just a matter of time before they found him, needle still stuck in his arm, eyes rolled back in his head, tongue swollen and slightly protruded; just another stiff.

Bubbles had been friends with Boyd for a long time, except for that Bubbs didn't really have friends because he didn't really care about anyone. He wanted so badly to be a drug dealer, Tony Montana in his own mind. But he was an idiot, and could really only inspire confidence in people like Ed.

But he always had dope, so we always let him in.

He wanted to introduce us to cocaine one day. Of course, Boyd and I were intimately acquainted with cocaine, but Bubbles didn't know that. We let him try to get us hooked on freebase. Boyd's father used to deal coke back in the day and he still liked to get down on occasion. And it's always been my favorite. But Bubbles didn't know that, either.

So, Bubbles and Eddie had the grand master plan to get us hooked on freebase cocaine, first few hits for free, and then jack up the price. Classic drug dealer move, at least on tv. But they had not counted on Boyd and me being connoisseurs of the coca leaf and its various incarnations.

Bubbles had bought himself an 8 ball, and probably about halfway through, he got the idea to make his money back and go buy another 8ball. So, he mixed it up with some baking soda and a little water and spread the paste over several tin foil sheets, 7 or 8, I think. He claimed he had dozens of foil sheets ready to go. He had in his drug-addled mind that he would smoke 1 sheet with us, and then get us to buy the rest of the sheets for $25 apiece or so.

Obviously, given our current state, we had no money for cocaine. If we were rolling like that, we would have had our own 8 ball and would not have answered the door when Bubbles and Eddie showed up. Nothing ruins a coke binge faster than an uninvited guest who wants in on the action. It's almost worse if they have brought an inferior product than if they show up empty handed.

And 2 lines worth of cocaine mixed up and

spread over a sheet of tin foil is definitely an inferior product, in my humble opinion. We were on the pin by that point anyway, so we were tweaking real fucking hard when we did come across the funds for a bender.

Anyway, Bubbles and Eddie show up with these sheets, touting the high quality of product and the superior method they had just invented for using said product. Boyd glanced at me, eyes twinkling in the reflection off the tin foil, and said,

"Well I've never heard of this...how about you, Jack? You guys know we don't really do cocaine very often...."

"Oh no," I responded, "why it's been months since I saw any cocaine. And I never, ever saw anything like this shit here. How does it work, Bubbles?"

"Well boys, it's like this. I call it chasing the dragon. What you do is, while someone holds the lighter under the foil, you inhale the smoke with this hollow Bic pen. Before you know it, you'll be just as fucked up as ole Ed here."

Randy, who was not really into heavy dope as much as Boyd and I were, harrumphed at the idea that Ed was any more fucked up today than any other time. Muttering under his breath about charlatans about to get ripped off, he headed into his room, slamming the door behind him.

Boyd and I knew Randy was not talking about us getting ripped off, he knew what we were up to. We were of course surprised that he knew a word like charlatan, but Bubbles called out after him,

"Fuck you Randy! Nobody's trying to rip anybody off!"

"So let's try it," Boyd quickly brought the conversation back to the task at hand. We smoked the first sheet, Boyd going first for about half of it, then me. Bubbs was right, he must have started with pretty good coke, because even after his dickery with the baking soda it was still decent. The shit would get you high.

You would never know it from watching Boyd and me, though.

"I'm not getting anything, Bubbs. Let me try again." Boyd kept saying. I could tell he was as high as a grocery bill on payday, but I played right along.

"Me neither. Maybe we need a better pipe," I said. Bubbles protested that we must not be hitting it right and that they had been smoking with that hollow pen all day and just look at poor Ed. But I floated on into the kitchen and cut the bottom off a 20 oz Mt. Dew bottle so we had a big, wide bottom pipe to pull through.

"Now we're cooking with grease!" Boyd exclaimed as he grabbed the soda bottle and commenced to sucking down as much smoke as I could create with 2 lighters going.

"Now we won't lose any smoke!" he exclaimed between puffs.

We were on sheet 5, still telling Bubbles that it wasn't working, and he was protesting the whole time that it wasn't right, what we were doing. But he was stuck in the Waiting Room, and there weren't a lot of choices for him.

There is no escaping here.

Randy had come out and joined us. Of course, he couldn't hide how fucked up he got off his first hit, and Bubbles started to really get upset because he finally figured out exactly what was going on.

He was delayed in doing anything about it because Randy, in the midst of the cocaine rush, picked up all 300+ pounds of Bubbles and body slammed him. From over his head.

Like Rick James said, cocaine is a hell of a drug.

Realizing that the cocaine gravy train was pulling into its final station, I did the only logical thing, and swung for the fences. Boyd was manning the two lighters and I was inhaling the biggest hit of my life when suddenly, the rushing in my ears got louder and louder and my peripheral vision got blurry and started to overtake my regular vision and I felt myself floating up and away while simultaneously falling backwards into the soft flabbiness of Bubbles, who was still trying to get up off the floor where Randy had body slammed him behind me.

The Nurse's whistle started soft and low, gaining in intensity until, BAM!

I woke up on the floor, looking up at Boyd's concerned face.

"Thought you were shuffling off this mortal coil... or at least through that door at the end of the hall," he mumbled, shaking his head.

"Are we out of coke? That shit was pretty decent," I managed to say with a weak smile.

Bubbles, with an utter disregard for my health and welfare, immediately pounced on my admission. He started blustering around, cursing us as he gathered up Ed and what was left of his last aluminum sheet. It was the one Ed had been quietly smoking on by himself, perched up on the edge of the love seat like a skinny, sickly gargoyle, laughing to himself at Bubbles's ongoing predicament.

We had forgotten he was there, which honestly, is when ole Ed seems to be most comfortable. He knew how to pass time in the Waiting Room.

They staggered off, with Bubbles warning us of the ill will we had just engendered through our mean-spirited trick and the dishonest way we had taken advantage of him. But with a lot more "fuck you guys" thrown in.

"Well," said Randy," That was fun. do you think he's coming back with any more of those sheets?"

"Oh, I'm sure he'll be back. They always come back. None of us can really stay away," Boyd said, searching furiously for a match to light his cigarette.

We had apparently killed both of our lighters chasing the dragon.

Four

Betty and the Corps

The way Staff Sergeant Jones came to the Waiting Room, is that the Marine Corps has this policy about drug tests; and they also apparently have this policy about quotas.

I had no business whatsoever being involved in the military. I generally don't agree with anything the military is ever doing. I generally have a very hard time following directions, let alone orders of any kind. I generally have a problem with authority. I generally am pretty lazy and avoid organized exercise at all costs. I smoke. I drink. I take all manner of drugs. I do all these things to the ab-solute utmost of my ability, usually only stopping when the money runs out, and only stopping then temporarily until I find some money. Also, I think I am smarter than virtually everyone I ever come in contact with, especially jarheads.

Boyd on the other hand, seemed like a natural fit for the military. He was strong, and in shape, and a dead shot, and good in the woods or wilder-ness, and good at camping and hiking and out-doorsy shit. He could hunt and track prey, and knew how to skin things, he could survive off the land. He knew about explosives and hand to hand combat, and guerilla warfare. Vital skills in time of armed conflict. Except for an independent streak and a drug habit, he was the perfect recruit.

I can only imagine the recruitment boner that SSgt. Jones must have gotten when Boyd walked into his office. This kid was already in camouflage, and was already heavily armed. Talking about: "I want to kill, sir!"

Yes, Boyd was the stuff the military's wet dreams are made of, a rabid redneck who can shoot the eye out of a running rabbit and is ready to shoot anyone and everyone if only given the order, or tacit permission. He had been talking to SSgt. Jones since junior year.

Boyd had probably been planning to join the Marines after graduation since junior year, although I never heard about it until after we wrecked the car. For Boyd, the Marine Corps offered a way to escape Bell County, a way to get away from the drug den he had grown up in, a way to really make something of himself.

Plus, he wanted to kill, sir.

Randy wanted to join for similar reasons. He was not college material and he knew it. He wanted to get away from his conniving conman father, and the memory of his dead mother. I think he partially thought of joining up as a way to do something honorable in memory of her. God knows she deserved it, if anyone did. So, around Christmas break of their senior year Randy committed too. That left me with the prospect of living in Hell's Waiting Room by myself, which was a commitment I was not prepared to make. I figured it wouldn't be much fun without them, and I was flunking out of college at a frighteningly rapid rate. So I joined too.

The problem, of course, was the drug testing

policy. Boyd joined earlier than Randy and me, he cleaned up for 2 weeks, worked out and flushed the drugs from his system, went with SSgt. Jones to Louisville and completed all the paperwork and official drug test. Smooth, like butter.

Not so with Randy and me. We cleaned up for 2 weeks, worked out and tried to flush the drugs from our system, went with SSgt. Jones to Louisville and failed our drug tests. SSgt. Jones was pissed, but he told us we would have to wait 30 days before we could reapply, and during that time we had to quit all drugs, especially marijuana.

When we made it back home from Louisville, before Jones was even out of the parking lot, we were lighting a joint. We did have 30 days to get clean after all, and we were stuck in hell's waiting room besides. And our piss was apparently already dirty.

Randy got right on it the next day, though. He was serious about it. He wore garbage bags over his clothes and would jog all around the neighborhood like an insane Rocky caricature. He didn't smoke after that first day, and when the 30 days was up, he was ready.

Not me. I smoked pot like it was my job for the

first 2 weeks of the 30 days. Boyd was no help. He had already passed his drug test so he was smoking pot again too. Besides, he could apparently clean up in 2 weeks or less. And Betty from upstairs had been bringing over that goddam homegrown weed she got from her nephew. We didn't trust it at first, having been told our entire lives that only white pot farmers could grow good dope. But we met her nephew's pot was just as good as anybody else's, except Boyd's father's. Boyd's dad grew the fire for sure, but Betty's nephew's shit was pretty fucking good.

Betty was in her late 50's, probably pretty hot back in the day. She had legs for days, and a nice smile, but this deep, gravelly voice from 1000 years of smoking. On the phone she sounded like a man, and was called Mister quite regularly. Boyd said if she hadn't been so hot, he would have sworn she was a transvestite. I didn't tell him that trans folks are quite pretty too. I figured he would have to find that out on his own, the old-fashioned way.

Betty was on disability from falling off the back of a garbage truck 10 years prior. Bad back. But the garbage company thought she was full of shit, so her case had been in litigation forever. She was going to get a payout someday she kept saying, and leave this shithole. She watched the weather channel at high volume, nonstop, either to drown out the noises emanating from the Waiting Room, or to cover up how she fucked Jefferson.

Jefferson was her sorry, no account boyfriend. Least that is how she introduced him to us the first time. She figured we were either drug dealers or skinheads when we first moved in.

In either case she was gonna find out about us. We had Darnell helping us move in, and Betty came strutting down the long wooden balcony that connected all the apartments, clicking and clacking her high heels, which she did not need since she was at least 6 feet tall without them.

"Oh my Lawd, who is that tall drink of water?" she croaked at us when Darnell appeared at the top of the steps holding the TV.

"And so strong too, honey!"

Darnell had that effect on black women, especially the older they were. Betty had Jefferson in tow, a suspicious scowl on his face.

"Look here, Jeffy, that's what a real man look like," she purred at Darnell, who blushed and took the TV in the apartment.

Being a lady, Betty did not follow him in, but perched on the balcony railing, her longass legs crossed ever so seductively. I was on smoke break, and cordially introduced myself since Boyd was off hiding to avoid work, and thus was unavailable to introduce us. Watching how Betty moved, it was pretty clear the garbage company was right, but she was nice enough.

"Another big one!" She exclaimed when she saw Randy emerge from the apartment.

"Ooo, Jeff, it will be like a backwards Oreo cookie!"

Jefferson looked uncomfortable at that prospect and mumbled something about going for a drink and ambled off down the stairs toward the corner bodega, about 3 blocks away.

"Jefferson used to be a good man, but he can't get it up no more without some help," Betty explained to me as she lit up a smoke.

"I have to rely on Big Blue most of the time." She held up her hands about 20 inches apart.

"That's my dildo, baby."

I decided I did not really want to talk about Betty's dildo anymore, but she was already into a story about breaking it out for Jefferson the other day, to try and help him get there. I did not see the correlation, exactly, being young and naïve to the sexual appetites of old people. I always figured that shit on the porno was staged to a certain degree.

But then Betty said,

"I slapped him with it and he said, 'OOO, and purred like a kitten." This seemed to conclude Storytime with Betty, much to my relief.

"Y'all got any pot, or are you skinheads?"

I explained to her that we were not skinheads, Randy and I had just recently had some bad luck with cutting our own hair, and that we did smoke weed, but we were dry at the moment.

"Well, your loss, I guess," she said, as she started to mosey on down the steps to the parking lot. She passed Boyd on the stairs, freshly returned from his hiding spot.

"You must be Boyd, I'll see y'all later when you get unpacked." And with that she was sashaying down the street.

"What the hell was that?" Boyd asked me when he got up the stairs to my smoking station.

"The neighbor. She's cool. Gonna smoke us up later. Ask her about Big Blue."

Betty became a regular in the Waiting Room. She always came over early, while she had her laundry going, which gave her a good escape plan to keep from getting trapped in there all day. Sometimes Jefferson would come too, but he didn't like the music. He was always asking if we had any smooth jazz.

Which of course we did not.

So, Jefferson didn't come that often, which suited Betty just fine; she thought pot contributed to his limp dick problem. And she needed dick all the time, she said, sexual prime and all that.

Betty always brought weed. It usually wasn't very good, unless it was her nephew's. Normally she had the brown frown we called it, Mexican pressed weed that she got from up the hill in Newberry Heights. Anyplace with New and Heights in its name is guaranteed to be ghetto. The only street name that spells ghetto more than that is MLK, or sometimes the low number streets.

Anyway, Betty had some people that lived up there, her family that had not moved uptown with her. Of course, uptown in Middlesboro, KY just means 4 or 5 blocks away. We all used the same bodega for fucks sake, at the bottom of Newberry

Heights hill. Anyway, she always brought some pot with her to hang out with these white dudes half her age and talk shit about her boyfriend, supposedly hoping for that backward Oreo sandwich.

But I think that was all a bit of a show, just Betty being Betty.

So, we were smoking some weed Betty had gotten from one of her other nephews in Newberry Heights, when SSgt Jones came calling. He had assumed, correctly, that I was not refraining from smoking pot. Not even a little bit of restraint. Of course, in my mind, the weed was just to help come down off the cocaine bender we had been on the night before, but square people like SSgt Jones don't understand shit like that.

We had a full Waiting Room when he showed up. Randy's brother was over. Sarah and Jessica were there from school. They were completely out of our league, but Sarah was friends with Boyd and had given him and Randy a ride home when they decided to ditch at lunch. Margot had stopped by, with a friend of course, to smoke some pot, and as per usual, Betty had come by. It is good that they had all come over to smoke. Otherwise, SSgt. Jones might have found only me and Katie, getting high and drawing on the walls. As it was, there were plenty of people to draw his attention away from me and the giant cloud of smoke I was exhaling when he entered the room.

It didn't work. He still noticed.

"Ladies," SSgt. Jones greeted the room.

"What the fuck is going on in here, Recruit?" he demanded, looking at Boyd and me.

"I can smell the goddam weed. Come on, we're taking a test right now."

Boyd protested that he was clean, and had already passed his test. Randy's brother, Little Bro spoke up for me, to assure SSgt. Jones that I too had clean pee. Everybody did, Little Bro said. I shot him a look, but I was trying hard not to laugh. I couldn't imagine what Jones thought he was going to find, barging up in here like that, but a smartass little kid like Little Bro was definitely not part of it.

"Now hold on, Mr. GI Joe Man," Betty cooed, as she unfolded out of the love seat and stretched up to her full height including 6-inch stilettos. Her tits were directly in SSgt. Jones's face, and he could not take his eyes off of them.

"These boys is good boys. They have not been

smoking any of my little bitty stash I got with me cause I'm stingy and don't like to share. What you smell is my very own special blend of herbs and spices, and if you that interested, my apartment is just upstairs and you can test out your GI Joe-kung-fu grip on this right here."

And with that she brushed her bosoms across his face as she spun around, slapped her ass, loudly, and sashayed out the door, trailing a long yellow and purple silk scarf behind her.

SSgt. Jones was at a loss for words. He stared after her, and then he stared some more. His eyes softened, he loosened his tie, and sat down on the edge of the couch, under the Sky Lizard's watchful eyes, with that old .45 pointed at his head, and exhaled sharply.

"Whooooowwweeeee," he said soft and low.

"That, right there, boys, is a woman. My God." And with that he leaned back on the couch, closed his eyes, and seemed to relax; the only time I think he may have ever relaxed. Without opening his eyes, he said,

"Boyd, you know that since you have already been accepted it will be a big deal if I test you now? And Jackie, you goddam drug addict prick, you're gonna fail again, aren't you? Don't answer that. Let me tell you a story…"

And thus began one of the longest and most interesting manifestations of the Waiting Room's power. SSgt. Jones opened up to three recruits and a room full of high strangers about his father, and how he was always riding him to follow in his and his grandfather's footsteps and join the Navy. But the water made him seasick. Always had. When he was a boy up in Maine, his dad would tie him to the sailboat, a Colgate 220, whatever the fuck that was, and sail around the harbor, threatening to go out into the open sea. All the while, young Jones is puking and crying and puking and crying, and wishing with everything in his little body that he could be somewhere, anywhere away from the sea.

So on his eighteenth birthday he joined the service, but the Marines instead of the Navy, just to fuck with his dad. They never spoke again, as his father was killed later that summer in a naval incident at sea. A new pilot fucked up his landing on the air craft carrier and took out everybody on the poop deck. Margot had just lit a bowl and passed it to Little Bro, who busted out laughing at "poop deck." Undeterred, and accepting a cigarette from Katie, SSgt. Jones continued his tale of woe.

He had never recovered from his father dying while they weren't on speaking terms. For all the childhood torture, he had a soft spot for the old bastard, and he had carried this burden from then on. He developed a taste for alcohol, he explained as Katie brought him beer, and Randy brought him a bottle of Jack Daniels and a tumbler. Jones filled the tumbler to the brim.

"Let me tell you something boys and girls, don't ever think you can drown your sorrows at the bottom of a gin bottle provided by Thai hookers. You'll end up in the brig, which is where I've spent my fair share of nights."

He explained that he had lost every good posting he'd ever earned, and was now stuck in the recruitment office of this "backwater shithole part of the country."

He sat up straight, looking around the Waiting Room, taking it all in, seemingly for the first time.

"There is something about this place you've got here, I can't put my finger on it. But I like what you've done with it. Very feng shui or something, makes you feel like we're all in this together, and at least we are in here and not out there. But seeing that vision, that stunning depiction of what God intended when he created woman, I've come to a realization. I need to find love. That's what's been missing in my life. Real love, from a real woman, a real lady, like your neighbor. My God."

And with that he jumped up off the couch, saluted the sky lizard and made for the door. He paused in the entrance when the sunlight blinded him upon opening the door. He turned to look over his shoulder at us, sipping our beer and watching his crazy ass.

"Jackie, don't show up to piss if it ain't clean, and Boyd we have to schedule you for a test in two weeks. Randy you're still on for two weeks too. Don't fuck this up. Now what is that lovely thing's name from next door?"

"Betty Baby, you sexy Marine Corps stud, you!" we heard Betty call through the wall, in her deep, gravelly voice. Jones looked back one more time, eyebrows raised, wondering if this was the voice of the same woman he had just been swept off his feet by. Boyd smiled, nodded, and waved SSgt. Jones out the door.

"Rice paper thin walls, I guess," I mumbled as I searched for my lighter and a joint.

"Fuck a drug test," I said firing up a doobie.

The next day, Betty gave us the scoop, which apparently was that she had rocked his world the night before.

"He talking about wanting to get married," she scoffed.

"I told him my momma ain't gonna let me marry no damn white boy, even a fine-looking military man like him. She'll come up out the grave to get me if I try some shit like that. I think I broke his little heart."

"Like you do to all the rest of us," Randy told her with a smile. He continued,

"It won't matter, I'm gonna ace my drug test whether you're fucking the recruiter or not. Might could help Jacko out though."

Randy was wrong, there was no helping me. I didn't even go to my test; I knew I wouldn't pass. Betty couldn't help Boyd either, he failed as well. Only Randy made it through the drug test.

Boyd and I decided it must not yet be our time to leave the Waiting Room, but Randy had a ship date to prove that it was possible to actually exit the Room. He was bittersweet about it.

I didn't tell anybody, but I didn't really want to leave anyway. I was content right where I was. And I realized there was no guarantee Randy would actually make that ship date anyway.

Five

Tweeker Dave

Betty hated Tweeker Dave. Tweeker Dave had lived in the building almost as long as her, but Tweeker Dave did not hang out. As the name suggests, he was always going ham on some kind of speed. We figured mostly meth he cooked in the apartment with his little jack russel terriers. He had 2 of those bastards, and you could hear them 24 hours a day. Back and forth chasing a tennis ball that Tweeker Dave would toss for them. Thump, thump, thump. Nonstop fun for the dogs. And normally, nonstop torture for the apartment below him, which was where we were.

We never really seemed to notice him though. The Waiting Room seemed to have its own sound-proofing, or the distractions were too great to pay attention to the neighbors. He was always coming and going, to and fro, all the time, ostensibly walking the dogs.

"There he go with them fuckin dogs again," Betty would say.

"I wish they would all just choke on that fuckin tennis ball and die!"

Of course, when she would see him on the stairs, it was,

"How you doin, Baby? Look at them cutey pies, sweetest dogs in this building!"

I guess white lies really don't hurt anyone. Better than choking a dog to death with a tennis ball, I suppose.

I only saw inside Tweeker Dave's pad once. He did not entertain company, as you might surmise. It started because Randy had found a key to the vending machines at the high school. Well, really, he saw the maintenance man set it down and he grabbed it as he walked by. Randy had quicker hands than you might think. It turns out that it was not a fully universal key, but it did open quite a few vending machines around town.

Never a cigarette machine, that would have been too easy. But we robbed several vending machines this way. The problem was, some of the change boxes themselves were locked. So, we would grab the whole box, if it was one that would come out, which most of them were, and bring it back home to break open.

Early one morning, we had been out all-night collecting boxes and were using a hammer and screwdriver to break into the boxes in the Waiting Room. On about box 4, Tweeker Dave starts beating on his floor/ our ceiling.

Guess he was finally trying to sleep. All he yelled out was,

"Why didn't ya use screws?!?"

"Good question," Boyd muttered as he pried the top off the box he was working on. We all laughed at the prospect of us hanging pictures on the wall at 3 am, or whatever Tweeker Dave thought we should have used screws for, and the next morning around noon I went upstairs to apologize. Tweeker Dave opened the door only a crack, mostly filling it with his skinny ass, dressed in only a wife beater.

Only a wife beater.

"Whatdya want?" he bellowed, dick quivering in the brisk morning air.

"Sorry about last night," I said, craning my neck to see over his shoulder. I was looking over his shoulder because I did not want to see his dick anymore, and, also, I wanted to see how Tweeker Dave was living.

I couldn't see much, limited as I was to the crack between the door and the doorjamb, and above his shoulder and below his dick. From what I could see, the entire apartment was stacked floor to ceiling with banker boxes, the ones you buy at Walmart or Staples and fold together yourself. Each box appeared to be meticulously labeled with its contents, long inventory sheets were stapled to the outsides of each box on all 4 sides. I suppose that was so no matter how he stacked them he could still tell what was in them.

There was a narrow, winding trail through the stacks that led toward the kitchen/lab, from which thick smoke was bellowing. The jack russels were completely unphased by the smoke swirling through the living room and out the open window, and appeared to be bouncing the tennis ball to themselves and chasing it incessantly. I guess when you go as hard as ole Dave does, you have the energy to teach your dogs to bounce their own damn ball.

"So.....whatdya got going on in here, Dave?" I started to ask as he shut the door in my face.

I decided this was too fucked up to not knock again, so I started knocking again. Tweeker Dave did not answer the door again, but instead started shouting through the door about all the banging around we were doing in the hall way every morning.

I believe he was referencing the work the maintenance man, Saul, was doing on the decking and staircases, replacing rotting boards with slightly less used ones he had scavenged from somewhere.

"Why didn't you use screws?!?" Tweeker Dave kept yelling through the door, punctuating each of his profanity laced tirades with this burning question.

Unable to get any clear answers out of Dave, I went off in search of Saul, to get to the bottom of this screw mystery. And to let him know that if

Dave burned the building down, would he come by and let us know?

You never knew about Saul. Saul had been in America forever, but was still working on the language it seemed. At least if he didn't like you, or didn't like the question, then he couldn't understand shit.

Saul had been a farm jeffe for 15 years until the immigration showed up. The jeffe's job was a coveted immigrant position on any farm. He was the guy who could speak English and bring in the non-English speakers to do the actual work. He told me he charged the farmer about $8 an hour per head, and he paid the workers about $7 an hour. So, every morning he would round up 50 to 60 migrant workers, mostly Mexican he said, and oversee their working on the farm. He had a whole system of drivers who did the actual transporting from the various Mexican neighborhoods, and they got $2 a head for driving the vans.

In a 10-hour day, after expenses, I figure Saul made about $500 during the growing season for organizing the whole thing, plus his hourly rate from the farmer of $10. It's good to be a Mexican sometimes, I guess. Until La Migra (ICE) raids the farm and fucks your shit up.

So now Saul was maintenance man for the apartments, but he still had that jeffe mentality. He was always bringing along helpers who seemed to do the bulk of the work, and he was probably still keeping a dollar or two out of their hourly pay from the landlord.

He seemed to pick his helper based on the helpers' sisters. He was always dating the helper's sister and I could never figure out if he was ditching his girlfriend when he ditched the helper, or if he was ditching his helper when he ditched his girlfriend.

We had gotten to know Saul a little bit because we figured a jeffe would know where to get some good cocaine through the Mexican community. Saul might have known, but he was not about to come off of that info to the likes of us. He claimed religion was the reason he didn't fuck with any drugs, and he did seem to be clean and sober, and religious. He had Our Lady of Guadalupe tattooed all big on his arm, so maybe religion was part of it.

But I figured he had realized that it was a lot

easier to stay off the radar if he wasn't really ever doing anything illegal, besides being Mexican. So, he did legal-like shit nobody else wanted to do, like be our maintenance man. Between him and his helper, they kept the place up good enough for our sort.

Saul's current helper was Fat Jose, whose sister was not as hot as Marco's sister had been. But Saul said Marco's sister was crazy, and she did always have that crazy look in her eye. So now we had Fat Jose.

Fat Jose and I had a special bond: we had heard a murder together.

Six

Bev's Wig

It was one of those warm spring mornings, when the sun is shining, the birds are chirping, the flowers are blooming, and a hooker is looking for you, interrupting your wake and bake. I had woken up early, and gone out onto the breezeway to smoke a roach, when I saw Bev coming up the street. Bev was a sometimes hooker, sometimes stripper, sometimes call girl. She was hot in a high-priced hooker kind of way, but I don't think the pricing was commensurate with her hotness.

She lived in our neighborhood, after all, and she still worked the corner on weekends.

Bev came by sometimes, usually wanting harder shit than we had to offer, but she would usually settle for smoking with us on her way to work. We knew better than to let a junkie hooker know we were holding anything better than pot.

It seemed early for Bev to be out and about, and she had 3 of her kids with her, the twins and the one with the big hair. Bev had her own hair under her blonde wig. The last time I had seen her in that wig was the time her pimp/boyfriend/fiancé/baby daddy was trying to drag her by it down the road. Of course, the wig came off and Monty threw it in the street, calling her everything but a strong black woman. She was cussing him too, and when her wig came off, she really went off.

She threw the littlest kid, who was only a year old or so at Monty, and I think that one was actually his because he made a great diving catch, and as he came up on one knee, she tried to impale his head with her stiletto heel by throwing an absolutely beautiful roundhouse kick.

I thought it was a pretty gangster move, distracting him with her own baby.

Lucky for Monty, she must have thought he was taller, or didn't know how high she could get that long leg up there, and her heel ended up barely grazing the top of his hat. We were out on the balcony, rolling, and Randy yelled,

"That's right, Bev, don't take no shit off nobody!" which got him a look from Boyd.

Betty just shook her head, toked the joint, and said,

"Dumbass motherfuckers, make us all look bad." Then she leaned way over the balcony and shouted down,

"You better leave that little girl alone, Montrell Hawkins! Don't make me come down there!" She then beat a hasty retreat to her apartment, muttering about how pulling a lady's wig off was fucked up, even if she is a whore.

Needless to say, I was surprised to see the resurrected blonde wig all cleaned up and back in the rotation. And early in the morning too.

"Hey Baby," she called out to me as she dragged the kids through the parking lot.

"Is your landlord around?"

She knew damn well that bastard didn't come

around there, he was not into checking up on any-thing.

"I heard they was an empty apartment around back."

There was in fact an empty apartment around back. These fast-assed kids had been using it as a trap house, near as we could tell, according to Betty. That's how we knew they was fast-assed kids, from Betty's description.

"I'm gonna go get a cigarette and a blunt, then come back and look at that apartment," she told me as she bounced off down the sidewalk, as if I had anything to do with renting her an apart-ment. I figured she and Monty must be getting evicted, or maybe he was kicking her out again, but I mumbled,

"Sure, whatever," and went back to smoking my joint.

I had just lit a cigarette, enjoying my buzz, when I heard a pop from down around back of the building. I looked down the balcony in the direction of the sound, and Fat Jose popped his head out of Old Man Brown's apartment. Old Man Brown was always bitching at Saul about his drafty windows, so I guess Jose was putting another piece of weatherstripping in there.

Fat Jose looked at me, I looked at him, he shrugged his shoulders, I shrugged my shoulders, and he disappeared back inside. I didn't think anything else about it, and eventually Bev arrived, with 3 of her kids, smoking her menthol and telling me to come with her around back to look at the apartment those damn fast-assed kids had just left.

Being stoned and bored, I thought, what the hell, it is nice watching Bev's ass shake while she struts and she always had her cleavage on point. So, we strolled on around the building toward the abandoned apartment, me watching Bev's ass, and her talking away about how they had to get out of that place they were in, rough neighborhood, etc. Of course, this was only a couple of blocks away, so it was still the same rough neighborhood, but whatever, I thought.

As we came up to the building, which had interior hallways rather than an open balcony like ours, I had a moment of chivalry and stepped ahead to open the hallway door. I threw open the door, and that's when I saw the blood. And the body.

There was a teen age looking kid lying in a pool of blood in the hallway floor. Bev stopped in the doorway, with the kids crowding around her legs to get a better look. I didn't know what to say, but I knew the kids probably shouldn't be there, so I said,

"Maybe you should come back later to see the apartment, Bev."

"Yeah," she said, "Yeah."

Turns out, the poor kid was set up by those very same fast-assed kids that used to live there. One of them sent him over to the trap house to get a bag, and the other one hid in the hallway behind the stairs and shot him. Stole his money and his chain, but not his cellphone.

The cops read the text messages, which led them to the first kid, who ratted on the shooter, and that was that. If there was any silver lining, Bev did come back later and rent the apartment. She might have been a hooker, and Monty might have been a dick, but at least they never shot anybody back there in the apartment.

Fat Jose didn't stick around though, not everybody can have a murder at work and still go in and punch the clock. Saul replaced him with Jesus, who they said was sort of like his cousin, whatever that meant in Mexico.

Jesus was a seedy little man, a former coyote who had brought a lot of Saul's family and work-force over.

Jesus got caught jacking off in the apartments, first thing. He was clearing out the apartment in preparation for Bev's move-in, and apparently, she had already started bringing some of her shit over.

Why she brought her sex boxes over first, I'll never know. Perhaps all her boxes were sex boxes. Anyway, Jesus was sent over to make sure it was cleaned out for the move-in, and he found the boxes full of porn and whips and toys and hand-cuffs and roleplay shit.

Bev said she was bringing the second load in when she caught him,

"Dickhanded, which mean he had his fuckin dick in his fuckin hand looking through my per-sonal shit! My personal, private shit, y'all!"

She threatened to sue and ended up getting half off the next month's rent.

We asked Saul if he could send Jesus over to

jack off in our apartment for half off the rent and he told us to eat a dick. Which caused us to all fall out laughing. Even Saul could tell Jesus wasn't going to work out long term as a maintenance man.

In addition to everybody bitching about him jacking off, Jesus didn't really like being a maintenance man, you could tell. Fixing broke shit for dickheads who are the same ones who broke it in the first place is not for everyone. He never smiled, and his beady little eyes were always darting this way and that, like the fucking roadrunner or something.

Little Bro and his buddy DooWop started calling him Wile E Coyote, which he definitely did not like. Saul came one night to ask Boyd and me to knock that shit off.

"Look, man, he used to be a guide, you know? Bring people across from Mexico. And now he is trying to leave that life behind and become a worker. Like me and like everyone, you know. Just tell your kids to leave him alone. He thinks people are going to find out who he is and come for him."

We assured Saul that those damn kids were definitely Randy's responsibility and that we would talk to him about it.

"Thanks," he said. "I don't want any trouble, I told Jesus he can only stay if the chollos don't find out where he is. You understand."

And with that he left us, wondering what a chollo was.

Seven

They made a movie out of it

It was around this time that we decided to make a movie. We had just seen Pulp Fiction, which led to backtracking onto Reservoir Dogs, and Boyd said,

"We could do that shit. I'm waaaay cooler than Vic Vega, and you're one bad motherfucker, motherfucker, so it could just be about us. We'd have a kickass soundtrack for sure."

It seemed like a good idea, especially if we let Randy have a decent amount of control over the music. He had a much broader appreciation for music than me and especially broader than Boyd. Boyd's soundtrack would have been Rage Against the Machine, Marilyn Manson, White Zombie, with a little Jim Croce and Bob Dylan sprinkled in.

But Randy was always bringing in old hippy music and folk rock his mom used to listen to. He'd play old punk, early acid rock, jam bands, newer weird shit, a little bit of everything. His playlists would have everything from Velvet Underground to Cake and Beck. Naturally there were staples like Zeppelin, Petty, and the Stones, but he'd slip some Ween in there and some Violent Femmes out of the blue. He could have put together a great soundtrack, no doubt in my mind.

Figuring that the music would be on point, and knowing that good music is obviously half of a good movie, we set about deciphering the film industry. The Blair Witch had made some money at that time, using only a camcorder, and Clerks didn't have extensive camera work, so we set out to get a camcorder.

After some extensive research over a bowl and a beer, we settled on stealing one from Eleanor. Eleanor was the Biology teacher at the high school, well hated by everyone the world over, but she was also the stepmom of Wee Boy Jimmy. I had met Jimmy at the academy I attended for high school. My mom worked there, so I could go for free, and they had a soccer team. Jimmy went there because his dad was a doctor and because Jimmy was little and got beat up all the time over at the public school.

A lot of the kids that came to the academy were that way, rich little snots who couldn't cut it at the big school. Anyway, Wee Boy Jimmy came my senior year and we became friends because we were both always sneaking off to smoke. He wasn't a bad guy, just sort of whiny and I could see how he would be a target for bullies, and why they used to call him Wee Boy Jimmy. Poor little feller.

But we let him hang around anyway, especially when Eleanor and Merv were going on one of their impromptu vacations. We would get wind of it and show up at Jimmy's house to party while they were gone. He was always supposed to be staying there alone, supervised by the perpetual grad student that lived in the basement, Charles from Edinboro. England. Charles was alright as a babysitter though, despite his penchant for chasing high school girls.

I don't think he ever caught one, so there were never any legal ramifications, mostly just creepy looks and rude commentary about any girl that graced the premises. Boyd and I had a talk with him on one of these weekends, and he started staying in his room more. I don't know how you say punkass in British, but that was what he turned out to be.

But as a babysitter, he was pretty cool. We would bring him a bottle of whiskey, and he would disappear. Eleanor and Merv never heard a fucking word from him about what went on while they were away. Jimmy didn't seem to mind much, as long as we kept it sort of low key.

It got out of hand the time we threw a party there while Jimmy was with Merv and Eleanor on vacation. Charles was back in England on holiday, so we had full run of the place for a week. The first day we didn't bring anyone over there, we just pilfered around, being nosy and looking through their stuff and eating their frozen pizzas. Drank all Charles's liquor stash too, but fuck him anyway.

This was when we learned a little about Eleanor's sexual preferences. She liked great big dildos with knobs and buttons and spin cycles. Also, apparently Merv wasn't up to snuff judging by the penis pump. We had a good laugh about it and decided Boyd and Randy would have no problem passing Biology from now on, should it come to that.

We didn't steal anything that first night, just inventoried it for later. The second and third night we had people over for a housewarming party in our temporary pad. As these things generally do, it got crazy. Too many people brought too many plus ones, everyone got too drunk, someone broke Eleanor's fancy glass statue thingy, and we probably did not clean up as well as we needed to, because Jimmy figured it out and was pissed.

We told him we would have invited him if he was in town, but it was no use. He didn't think we were his friends anymore. Which wasn't a stretch since Pavo and Randy really, really didn't like him anyway.

So, when we needed a camera and knew where Eleanor kept her camcorder and knew how and when to break in, it seemed like a no-brainer. We figured we could give her a spot in the credits when the movie took off, some sort of key grip of dildos reference or something.

Randy started narrating before we ever got the damn camera. The whole way over, while we were inside the house, everything. Despite their house having been stolen for a party the previous summer, they had not updated the security system at all, and Jimmy's little brother had been telling everyone all week at school how they were going to Hilton Head for Spring Break, the whole family.

They were still leaving windows unlocked and the basement door still did that trick Jimmy had showed me. Luckily, Charles was also away, because according to Randy's narration, it was not going to go well for him if he was there housesitting.

Randy ran the music for the caper, at least while we were in the car, and it would have been a great soundtrack, he told us, leading into the heist with CCR's Run through the Jungle, and the Specials Concrete Jungle for the getaway. It's going to be a jungle film, I guess.

So now we had a camera, ready to make the great American movie. We had delusions of grandeur, of course, figuring we would be on a par with Easy Rider, but with Dazed and Confused thrown in and some Natural Born Killers sentimentality throughout. But with no real plot in mind, we decided it would be better if it was more like Clerks. As Boyd put it,

"If anyone could hear the shit we say, they would crack the fuck up."

The problem was that Randy couldn't forget about the camera being there, and was constantly talking to it. When he wasn't posturing in the background of everything, or sitting right beside it narrating what was going on.

It got weirder and weirder over the course of a weekend, as he began to lie to the camera, telling of exploits that we had not done, and grossly embellishing the ones we had. And he would pull me aside to talk behind the camera's back, like he didn't want it to know the real story.

He got it in his head that we needed to present a more extravagant picture of ourselves, for the good of future generations who would view this film to learn about us, a sort of what makes these now famous petty criminals tick? How did they become the envy of every male in America, how did they get to be so cool?

So, he talked up our past exploits, and wanted to do repeats of the same conversation when he would think of something clever to interject. It was weird, and didn't really go with the idea of just letting the camera catch random, funny, and candid moments in Hell's Waiting Room. He started talking about how important this work we were doing was.

For the future he said. But also, he said,

"We have to be careful because we don't want them to know everything. We have to make sure to watch what we say, and who we say it to...."

The best parts of the film were undoubtedly the ones filmed by Randy's little brother. Little Bro came to stay for a couple of days periodically, when the dad would go to the casino to gamble away the mom's death insurance money. He was a piece of shit that way.

Anyway, Little Bro was one hell of a cameraman. He had a real knack for being in the right place at the right time, and contrary to his brother's narration, his was actually funny. Good sense of humor for a 10-year-old, but of course the pot was helping with that.

The day the camera died didn't start as that kind of day. I awoke to Randy talking to the camera about how our lifestyle would help to save the world, if everyone could just get past their differences and spend some time in Hell's Waiting Room, the rest of it would all make sense and we could survive the Holocaust. I never found out which Holocaust he was talking about, The Holocaust perpetuated by the Nazis, or some other one he had in mind.

It was all part of his new plan to convince future generations of viewers that we were benevolent geniuses with good manners, geniuses who would save the world. It was starting to rub off on me.

I had been having a nightmare where Little Bro was Bill, Randy was Ted, Boyd was Rufus, and we were in that fucked up bar from Star Wars looking for a flux capacitor to power the Death Star so we could save earth from total annihilation by the guys from Tron. The blue ones had turned on us, apparently.

I woke up in a cold sweat, worried about wattage.

I started digging through the ash tray to smoke a roach or two while I waited on Boyd to wake up, with Randy droning on and on to the camera. As the pot settled in, I decided to tackle Randy's crazy head-on. I explained to him, that all of this shit was unnecessary, because since we were the ones recording it, we could be the ones to edit it. We didn't need to talk around the camera as if it had a mind of its own. We could edit it for the time capsule or whatever the fuck he thought we needed to edit it for, to prove to future generations whatever the fuck he was trying to prove to them.

"After all," I concluded, "it's not like the cameras that are watching us from the satellites. We can control this one."

That was all it took.

Apparently, it had never occurred to Randy that the satellites could see him, if they really wanted to. And record him, if they really wanted to. Never thought about that shit while he was jerking off, and it showed.

He turned the camera off, set it on the pile of

garbage on the coffee table, and stumbled to his room, mumbling,

"What are we gonna do, they know everything..."

It turns out the thing to do in these situations, when you have just realized that we are not in control of our runaway technological advancements and that in fact much of your life and everything around you is controlled from afar, when you realize Big Brother is alive and well and watching your ass, the thing to do, apparently, is to make your friend who shared this fascinating nugget with you take you to Walmart to steal some tin foil for a hat.

A total buzzkill. Boyd yelled to bring back some tacos as we shuffled out the door, Randy in full Unabomber attire to conceal his identity from the satellites. The whole way over to Wally World, he's watching the sky, trying to spot those bastards and talking about how we need to build a hot air balloon or steal a jet or something that we can use to get up there to start shooting the satellites down.

I don't think hot air balloons really go into space, I wanted to say, but I did not belabor the point. At this stage, I was just hoping to get him off the streets before he tried to start a revolution.

And also, I was

figuring out how to tell him that I was not going in with him to steal the foil.

"You're on your fucking own, you crazy fuck," is what I went with.

When we arrived back at the apartment, Randy already had his hat done and had Little Bro's halfway done. Little Bro and Katie were over by the dumpster watching a fire they had going in the recycle bin. Boyd yelled down from the balcony about fucking tacos again, to which I replied,

"We got bigger problems right now than fucking chalupas."

"No shit!" Boyd bellowed. "Tell them what you told me, Little Bro, goddammit."

I turned to Little Bro, who was having his tin foil hat adjusted by Randy to fit properly, and he sheepishly explained how he had been climbing up the balcony to the roof, to try to see how pigeons fuck, and to see if he could film it; he had wanted to make like a pigeon fetish porn we could sell.

I was a little surprised that a 10-year old knew about fetish porn, and that he was interested in making one, although honestly, I shouldn't have been surprised by anything at that point.

Apparently, he slipped, and dropped the camera when he caught himself, and it fell the 3 stories to the gravel parking lot. The camera was smashed up pretty good, he said, and he got scared. He knew we would be pissed, and since we couldn't watch the video anymore because it was on that little tape that only fit in that camcorder, he decided to get rid of it all.

So Little Bro and the Katie decided to set the whole thing on fire in the recycling bin. It is unclear, at this point, how much input Katie really had since she didn't really talk. But between the two of them, they settled on a course of action and followed through with it.

Boyd was pissed, of course; and we had not brought any tacos.

But we realized it was probably for the best...you always end up having to burn the incriminating tapes anyway.

In the end, after enough tacos that we finally went and got for Boyd, we decided the movie didn't do it justice anyway.

It would have had a kickass soundtrack though.

Eight

Free DooWop

DooWop lived down the street, younger kid. His momma, Chicago Shelly, said they were from Chicago. Randy met her at the laundromat. Why he was at the laundromat remains a fucking mystery. They apparently got to talking about Randy's mom, which is where every conversation with strangers eventually ended up.

Randy was so sad. We tried to help him, as best we could, with a steady diet of uppers and downers and pot in between. We were always striving to achieve that elusive state of wellbeing and contentment, while staving off the fits of psychotic depression. Randy was fucked up pretty bad about his mom's suicide.

So, when he met DooWop's mom, and she started talking about having to leave Chicago because her oldest boy Leonard just died, Randy skipped over all about how and why Leonard had died, and went straight to,

"We are the same, you and me. We both lost a loved one recently. Come on over to my house any time," he had told her.

It mattered why Leonard had died, because he got shot robbing one of their neighbors. Apparently, Leonard had a little bit of a history, according to DooWop. Leonard had robbed just about everybody in their neighborhood, thieving bastard that he was, according to DooWop. Leonard learned that shit from their Daddy, Everett, who also was a thieving bastard, according to DooWop.

Doo Wop had shown up instead of his Momma a few minutes after Randy had returned home.

"I'm DooWop from down the street, my mama said you said to stop by anytime and I was wondering if you had any Dr. Pepper?" he had announced when Boyd answered the door.

"How old are you, kid?" Boyd asked him, door opened just enough for him to see who it was, but not wide enough for that person to see the sawed-off shotgun he had pressed up against the other side. When I had asked, he said he figured it might buck his arm out of socket, but if he needed to shoot somebody through the door, he'd take his chances.

"I'm sixteen, sir. My momma said you wasn't pervy, but I'll fuck you up if you try anything. And besides being a thieving bastard, my Daddy is a murderin' son of a bitch too!"

"And you are not 16!" Randy smiled cheerily as he came down the hall. "Let him in Boyd, this is the son of that nice lady I was telling you about. Little Bro is here for the weekend. They're the same age. I told his mom he could come over. They just moved here, and since he and Little Bro are gonna be in the same class and all..."

Boyd swung the door open, saying simply,

"Keep your hands to yourself in here, little buddy."

Randy gave Boyd a glare, and brought a new soul into the Waiting Room.

I don't think Randy intended to do this, you

understand, Randy just sometimes seemed to look at the bright side of things, instead of the side we were on.

I don't know how old DooWop really was, but he knew what was going on. He walked over to the ashtray, first thing, and plucked a big fat blunt roach out of it. He held it in his lips and reached into his pocket for a lighter, sort of grinning at me as I sat on the couch watching this fascinating turn of events. I glanced over at Katie, who was smiling in an almost grotesque fashion, eagerly anticipating what was bound to happen.

Out of the blue, Boyd sprang over the couch, narrowly missing Katie's head, which she held perfectly still, and landed precisely in front of DooWop, who was slowly raising his lighter from his pocket. Light flashed off Boyd's blade in a blur as he sliced through the roach, millimeters from DooWop's face.

DooWop realized it much too slowly, and only jerked his head back after the blade was already on its descent, being folded and placed back in Boyd's pocket in one fluid motion. Only faster than fluids could ever possibly move; Boyd was good. He caught the severed portion of the roach as it fell with his off hand, placed it in his mouth, and asked DooWop,

"Got a light, little buddy?"

To which DooWop sort of fainted and fell back into the couch under the Last Supper next to me, and the room erupted in laughter. Katie was rolling back and forth on the couch, Little Bro was dying in the corner, Betty was cackling that low, gravelly, laugh she's got; even Randy was laughing and I thought he might have gone the other way with it, on account of Boyd brandishing a weapon at his guest.

But shaking his head, Randy said,

"He fucking told you to keep your hands to yourself, DooWop."

DooWop had started to come around, and looking this way and that, his eyes finally rested on his own hand, which still clutched his lighter. Flicking the flame, he leaned forward and held the lighter up toward Boyd. Boyd bent over and lit his roach, which was too small to really safely light this way, yet somehow Boyd pulled it off without setting his face on fire.

He took a long pull, inhaled and handed the joint down to DooWop.

"Thanks for the light, but next time keep your hands to yourself in here, man."

DooWop nodded, and settled back into the couch with the roach. When he asked to use the roach clips, we knew he was one of us. Little Bro came over and sat on the couch next to him.

"Those roach clips suck," he said. "Next time we'll use mine."

DooWop nodded, passed him the roach, and became one of the community.

The Waiting Room was like that. Anyone could, and probably eventually would, join the group. There were no discriminations, no judgements, no requirements, none of that shit. Age didn't matter, gender didn't matter, socioeconomic status didn't matter, none of it mattered. If you were supposed to be there, you were there. Until your time was up, and you went back through that door, we were all in this shit together. And we were going to make the best of it.

DooWop stayed for days and days. He explained they called him DooWop because he loved to dance. He was a dancing fool, as they say, always bopping and grooving to whatever kind of music Randy played. He told us all about how fucked up his family was, how his dad and older brother were the stealingest black dudes he ever met.

"And it's not cause we're black," he said one night, almost out of nowhere. It had been two days since he had made the "stealingest black dudes" comment. Old black Betty had raised her eyebrows when he said it, but she didn't disagree. She had met the father, she said, and he was a no-good thieving motherfucker. People would always tell you what they really thought, when they were in the Waiting Room. At this point, what's the use in hiding anything?

DooWop continued,

"My Uncle told me y'all racist white folks in the South would think we was stealing cause we're black, but in Chicago we know y'all white ass crackers steal just as much shit as the rest of us."

"Did your Uncle tell you how many of us are racist, down here in the South?" I asked, genuinely curious.

DooWop nodded.

"He been living down here a long time. He said all y'all motherfuckers."

Katie nodded her pasty white head in agreement, but Boyd said sagely,

"Your uncle is mostly right. A lot of these white ass crackers is pretty fucking racist, man, so you do have to be careful. But in this place, we are not. And you let me know if you have any problems out there with the white devils."

DooWop nodded again, and went back to smoking a cigarette and dealing blackjack to Katie. She'd tap for a hit, get excited or flustered, depending on the card, but never utter a word. That girl never said anything, it seemed like.

And her poker face was awful.

They were playing for cigarettes, and DooWop appeared to be in the lead. Didn't really matter. Randy and I had stolen a case of cigarettes out of the Kmart the other day, so smokes were free for everybody.

"Camels, the wise man's choice," Randy had said at the time. I did like Camels, that's why it was the case I grabbed. Randy was on lookout, so I got to pick. Fuck his Marlboros, anyway. And Boyd truly did not care. He thought all cigarettes were basically worthless pieces of shit, except Camel Turkish Special Blend Silver, which were virtually nonexistent in our neck of the woods. But anytime we were in the city....

"Should we send DooWop home at some point?" I asked Boyd one morning as we walked over to the bodega to get some coffee. Our coffeepot was still on the fritz from overuse and Randy's attempted rewiring.

"I mean, with Little Bro gone home for the school week, isn't it kind of weird that he's still staying over? He's a little kid, for fuck's sake. Where are his parents?"

Boyd snorted and gave me a look of wry amusement.

"What are you, fucking family services now? C'mon, man. Maybe he needs to stay there. Maybe shit is fucked up at home. Betty said yesterday that Everett was on the run for robbing the Shell station again. They had suspected him for when it got hit last week, and this time the clerk is positively identifying him."

"Shoot'em'up Shell, over on Catalpa?"

"That's the one. Where Ivan put in the video surveillance."

Ivan knew everything there was to know about computers, as far as we could tell. He lived above his grandmother's garage on 22nd Street, after he got out of prison. Ivan had gone down when he robbed the Radio Shack after he installed their security system.

Unfortunately, the store assistant manager, who had eyes on being a store manager someday, was fooling around with the home video surveillance equipment in the floor model display. He ended up recording Ivan and his buddy Seth robbing the place blind.

To Ivan's credit, he never gave Seth up.

Ivan was out on parole now, and was not allowed to work on security systems or computers as part of his release. Had to wear an ankle monitor, which of course he figured out how to hack. He still did security camera installs, but only for halfway shady bodegas and gas stations who were not really vetting their vendors.

Ivan would come over every couple of weeks with a trunk full of computers to work on. Clearing the hard drives to resell them, is what he called it. We had no idea if that was even a thing, but we did understand cocaine, which was what he always brought as tribute.

"They have more trouble out of those cameras over there at the ole Shoot'em'up," Boyd concluded as we stepped into the bodega down the street from the Waiting Room, the Uphill Market. Their cigarettes were overpriced, but the cappuccino machine was on point. And they were the only place in reasonable walking distance for either of those two things.

They didn't rely on security cameras at the Uptown Market. They relied on bulletproof glass, and a shotgun if you got past the glass.

"So, what do we do about DooWop?" I asked again.

"I don't know man, maybe Randy should talk to him. He brought him in there in the first place."

I agreed that it was Randy's runaway, so he should have to deal with it. Somebody had to be the adult around there, and it sure as shit wasn't me.

As it happened, we ran into Chicago Shelly on our way back to the Waiting Room.

"Is my DooWop at your house?" she asked as we passed on the sidewalk.

"Y'all friends with Randy? You know that boy need help. Is he talking to someone, like a professional?"

"Yes, yes, of course," Boyd told her, skipping over the part where she somehow knew who we were. Of course, I suppose 'two crazy looking white boys in this neighborhood, walking around like they ain't got a care in the world' could have only been us.

Boyd continued,

"Margot's father is a doctor and has referred Randy to the finest specialists in the tristate area."

It was true. Randy had been to a few head shrinkers, even talking on the phone to the one recommended by Margot's father. I shudder to think of what that conversation was like. All we got out of Randy was that he wasn't allowed to call anymore.

Head shrinkers never worked out for Randy. The only ones he could get into through his Dad's Bible College were Christian Counselors who had no frame of reference for the shit we were doing. Sure, they might know about Randy's mother's suicide, and maybe suicide in general, but they had no idea how to talk to Randy when he started in on the Lizard People and the Demons and the Dreams he only had on huffing paint but never had on acid and why is that doctor? Shouldn't they be better on LSD? And where is God in all this?

These holy social workers were no match for a drug addled nutcase like Randy.

And real doctors cost money. Unless it is through the court system, and nobody should want to be treated by a court ordered head shrinker. So, until we came up with enough money for a proper psychiatric evaluation, we did our level best to keep Randy out of trouble with the law, and out from under court ordered psychiatrics.

Realizing that Chicago Shelly probably cared more about the answer to her first question than her last question, I said,

"Yes Ma'am, he is over there. Him and Randy's little brother have been hanging out a lot." Truth be told they were becoming virtually inseparable. I asked politely,

"Do you want him to come home?"

"Only if he wants to and you need him to. I got a houseful over there now. And with Everett wanted for questioning, he ain't been around. You know he didn't have nothing to do with that shit at the Shell station." This was contrary to all reports, including his own offspring, but I didn't argue with her.

"Just send him home whenever," she said as she ambled off towards the bodega.

"Well, I guess that answers that," Boyd said, and we didn't worry about DooWop's home situation anymore.

Until Everett came looking for him. The cops had caught up with him after a week or so, and hauled him in for questioning. Person of interest and all that. They only held him 24 hours. You couldn't break Everett in only 24 hours behind an armed robbery charge with no real eyewitness.

The clerk could only say for certain it was a black man with an enormous handgun. And the video from Ivan's security cameras was shoddy. They had to cut him loose.

Betty alerted us to Everett's presence in the alley before he ever made it up the stairs to our second-floor unit.

"That thieving ass motherfucker Everett is coming over here looking for DooWop," she said to Randy when he answered the door to her insistent knocking.

"I'm going to hide my shit off the porch and lock my doors. Thieving ass motherfucker."

Randy came back into the waiting room and

sat down, turning his attention back to Cheech and Chong. It was the part where they're rocking out with their band and Chong is all fucked up.

"Who was that?" Boyd asked.

"Betty. Said Everett is looking for DooWop."

"Shit." DooWop muttered as he started gathering up his cigarettes and lighters. Little bastard could play some blackjack. He'd gotten us for 4 packs of smokes already, plus Randy's zippo, and a pair of brass knuckles. And that's not counting what he took off the guests.

"I'm gonna hide, if that's all right with everyone. Just tell him I already went home."

Randy hadn't had enough to drink yet to pull off lying to strangers, and Boyd was headed to the shitter, so I had the honor of answering the door.

"Whose house is this?" Everett demanded when I answered the door.

"The Bank's," I said. He looked confused by my answer, so I tried to explain,

"You see, in today's fast paced economy a lot of people are looking for a good long-term investment, and multifamily real estate is just the ticket. Interest rates are at an all-time low, which means money is cheap for qualified individuals. The tenants pay your mortgage to the bank, and you can have the whole thing paid off in fifteen years as an investment that only grows over time. If we've learned anything in the past half century, it's that real estate values go up, up, up, so get in now while the circumstances are favorable."

I had watched an infomercial a few weeks ago on real estate investment, airing of course at about three am. Cocaine is a hell of a drug.

I continued, off script this time,

"But technically, though your name appears on the deed, keep in mind that until it's paid off, like any mortgage, it really belongs to the bank." At this I lowered my voice, and glanced nervously around, making sure no one else could hear this next secret tidbit I was laying on him.

"It's all just a ploy to get young suburban white folks with a little bit of a nest egg to pump their money back into the market so the banks can play with the funds on short yield stocks and bonds." I nodded my head sagely at him, and said,

"All in the game, brother, all in the game."

"Boy, what in the fuck are you taking about? Is DooWop here or not?" Everett looked confused by my explanation, and a little pissed about it.

I, for my part, had opened the door fully in a show of welcome, which was a mistake in retrospect. Should have gone with the Boyd shotgun technique, because Everett decided for some undecipherable reason to try to push past me and on into the Waiting Room.

I stood my ground, but the slippery little bastard stutter stepped me out of my shoes, and was in the home stretch when I heard the telltale click of Boyd cocking the hammer on his Browning 9MM. Everett heard it too, and stopped dead in his tracks.

"Beelzebub owns this domicile my friend," Boyd said, icy cold.

"And you are not welcome here. Being from Chicago, you might not be aware that they let folks shoot black men if they come in your house down here. Usually no questions asked."

Everett stuck his hands up in front of him, palms out and started backing away, mumbling about misunderstanding, and not wanting any trouble.

I held the door for him, telling him as he passed,

"DooWop already left."

I slammed the door behind him, locking the deadbolt and sank down into the comforting embrace of the couch, under the watchful gaze of the Lord's Supper and the Sky Lizard.

"What the fuck was that, man?" Little Bro asked Doowop as he emerged from the kitchen. DooWop had been under the kitchen sink with the bread bags. Randy always saved the bread bags, as they were the best for paint huffing. And every time we did paint, I was glad he had the foresight to save those damn bags.

"What am I gonna do, what am I gonna do?" DooWop wailed, obviously distraught over Everett looking for him, and what that might entail.

"Your momma said you can stay as long as you want. They married?" Boyd quizzed him.

DooWop shook his head, tears forming in his eyes. Marriage generally made custody battles more difficult, but I felt we were getting a little ahead of ourselves.

"He's gonna make me start helping him, now that Leonard is gone. Fuck, shit, fuck," DooWop lamented.

"And I don't want to. Fuck that shit. I can steal if I have to, but he's always wanting to do it for nothing. And he don't even use real bullets in the gun and he's gonna make me go in there cause they are figuring out what he looks like cause he only robs Shell stations cause my mom's name is Shelly and he thinks they stole the name in the first place. He's fucking crazy, and I don't know what to do. Maybe I should just run away."

Katie, the experienced runaway, was nodding her head in agreement, sure that running away from home was always the best option in times like these. But Randy was having none of it. He sat DooWop down on the couch, got him a cigarette and a beer, and told him,

"I'll talk to your parents about it. Don't worry."

DooWop managed a weak smile, but he looked unconvinced. Luckily, at that moment, Katie's timer dinged and it was time to take the pot brownies out of the oven.

We decided the thing to do was have a brownie and relax our troubles away; at least we figured that's what DooWop should do while we tried to sort out a solution. He was just a kid after all.

Later that night, Boyd and I sat on the porch with Betty, trying to formulate a plan.

"Well you could shoot him next time goddammit," Betty kept saying. "Thieving mother-fucker."

We figured that was always on the table, but we decided to try talking to them first. We agreed that Randy and I would go meet Chicago Shelly and Everett the next day and try to talk about a solution.

We never got the chance, as we awoke to quite a commotion going on in the parking lot at the disturbingly early hour of 9 AM. Everett had gathered all his people who would help him, which turned out to be about six individuals. They were marching in a little circle, chanting "Down with Beelzebub!" and "Release the Boy!" A couple of them had signs that read FREE DOOWOP.

"Jesus." Was all Randy could say.

"This is fucking trippy," Little Bro said grinning from ear to ear. He continued,

"A real live protest. When do the riot police show up with the tear gas? I'll get the gas masks," and he hurriedly began digging through Randy's closet.

DooWop was watching through the blinds on Katie's window she used instead of the door. We had offered to give her a key, although someone was usually there to let people in. She just seemed to prefer crawling through Randy's window to get in and out of the apartment.

"I was afraid this would happen," DooWop said sadly.

"Can I borrow the phone?"

He took Katie's phone when she handed it to him, and went into the kitchen and under the sink with the bread bags.

"This is fucked up," I said to Boyd as we watched from the porch.

"What is DooWop doing?"

"Under the sink, I guess. I think he's calling his mom. Or maybe social services," Boyd answered, and I found myself wishing I had brought a joint out to help lift the spirit of these melancholy proceedings. The cops showed up before Little Bro could find all the gas masks, but it didn't matter because they weren't riot police with tear gas, just regular cops.

We wandered out onto the porch so we could hear them. They started to ask Everett and his group what they were up to, but before he could go into what we could only assume would be a tale of the white devil holding his young son hostage,

DooWop appeared from out of nowhere, running up and embracing his father. He hugged him tight, telling him he loved him and missed him and was glad he was there.

It was a tender moment, and almost brought a tear to my eye. But then the strangest thing happened. The police officer by the squad car walked over, talking on his headset and looking quite concerned. He conferred with his partner, then they asked Everett to let go of DooWop and come downtown with them to answer some questions.

Everett started to protest, and then argue, and then run. He juked the first cop out of his shoes too, so I didn't feel so bad, but the second one caught him in a shoulder check that knocked him into Jefferson's shitbox Oldsmobile he had parked out there on blocks. Everett bounced off and hit the ground, hard. He lay there motionless as Jefferson hollered from Betty's window,

"You scratched my paint you cocksuckers! I want all your badge numbers!" Jefferson's only true pleasure in life was to yell at cops.

Everett lay motionless on the ground, the wind knocked out of him, while the cop cuffed him and searched him. The cop held a large automatic handgun up for his partner to retrieve, apparently found in Everett's waistband.

"No shit," Boyd said. "What are the chances?'

When the cop held up his hand again for his partner, we realized the chances were pretty fucking slim that this was coincidence. Clutched in his hand was a bread bag, wonder bread from the looks of the packaging. Randy's favorite.

"What have we got there?" the first cop asked, grinning ear to ear that the suspect hadn't gotten away and seemed to have copious amounts of contraband on him. Whether that was the gun from the robbery or not, a felon like Everett wasn't allowed to carry it. And the bread bag contained... a little Ziplock baggy, which contained...

"Cocaine," the cop confirmed, "About a half gram or so, looks like. Well, well, well, Mr. Everett. Looks like you are not as reformed as the Chicago parole board led us to believe down here in the Bluegrass state."

As the cops hauled Everett away, DooWop looked sad and forlorn, until the cop cruiser rounded the corner, at which point he broke out into the biggest of toothy grins. He laughed his way up the stairs and into the Waiting Room where he plopped down on the couch under Jesus.

"Alright, young man, what the hell just happened?" Randy demanded.

"Well, it's like this," DooWop began as he lit a joint, grinning ear to ear.

"I called the cops from Katie's phone and I figured he would bring a gun since Boyd pulled one on him yesterday. And I figured it would be the same one from the robbery because he is too cheap to get another one. And the bread bag of coke I slipped into his pocket just in case. I knew they'd find something as big as a bread bag," he said laughing.

"Where the fuck did you get a bread bag of coke?" Boyd asked.

I knew where it came from by the way Katie smiled, cocked her head to one side, and shrugged. And I knew DooWop wouldn't have to worry about her saying anything about it, ever.

"Told you I could steal if I had to. I just don't want to steal for that motherfucker. Can I stay here for a little while longer?" DooWop asked, opening one eye to gauge our response.

We agreed he could stay, and we agreed he

had probably done the best thing overall, and that Everett would probably always figure them bastard cops had planted that shit on him anyway.

DooWop's momma came around a few days later saying it was alright for him to come back home, Everett was denied bail and wasn't going to beat the rap this time. But DooWop still spent the majority of his time in the Waiting Room. He was part of the community, in there with the rest of us, making the best of what we had to work with.

And it was always better in the Waiting Room than out there through the door.

Nine

Willem

Mute Katie had been hooking since she was a kid. Ten or so, we found out later, from Willem. Ivan had brought his neighbor, Willem, with him when he showed up with a load of laptops and hard drives to scrub.

We knew Willem a little bit, we thought. He was a football starter, played both ways, linebacker and center. I always thought center would be a bit weird to play, what with the quarterback's hands up in your business from behind in your little tight spandex pants, giving you signals through little taps and pats on your inner thighs.

But football is the manliest of all our gladiator sporting events, so I never mentioned this to any football players, especially the center.

Willem was a pure country redneck, Mack truck hat, caterpillar boots, the whole bit. He ran with the other beer swilling misogynistic jock crowd that we typically only saw at parties and the like. It had not occurred to us that someone like Willem would grace our abode, but the Waiting Room was like that; you never really could be sure who would or would not end up there.

"Hey Boys!" Willem bellowed as he followed Ivan through the door.

"Randy, you look as sharp as ever!"

Randy hated Willem. Willem and some of the other jocks had given Randy a hard time freshman year, before he started hanging with Boyd. Typical high school shit, swirlies and wedgies and stuff like that. Randy was far too into music and art to escape the wrath of the uncultured brutes who inhabit the typical American high school. He would try to fight back, but he was no match for Willem and his cronies.

Until he met Boyd. Boyd had a gift for hand to hand combat, honed through a lifetime of fighting his father, Hippy John. Despite his moniker, Hippy John was about the furthest thing from what you expect a hippy to be. I guess it was one of those ironical type nicknames. Anyway, he beat the piss out of Boyd for years and years until Boyd got big enough to effectively fight back. At which point Hippy John resorted to knives and firearms. Boyd's arms and hands were covered with scars from defensive wounds and his ears constantly rang from Hippy John firing guns right next to his head. He liked to use the high Cal for that, he felt it was more intimidating.

The end result was that Boyd turned into a lean, mean, fighting machine. When the occasion called for such a thing. Consequently, nobody fucked with Boyd, not even the jocks, and the few who had tried were a permanently scarred bunch. One kid who had tried to jump Boyd still couldn't use the fingers in his right hand, Boyd having severed all the tendons with his knife. Another kid ended up blind in one eye from when Boyd shattered his eye socket. Another kid would always have a limp after Boyd bent his knee all the way the wrong way. Twice in one sitting.

So, the rest gave Boyd a wide berth, as well as anybody like me or Randy who joined in with Boyd's merry crew.

Boyd was not content to let his reputation speak for all of us though. We spent hours and hours in hand to hand training, knife fighting, firearm training. Boyd could take the sorriest sack of useless pudge and turn him into a badass, help him become a much more capable and dangerous version of himself, unlock that hidden potential for violent proficiency.

And that is what he did with Randy. After about a year, nobody fucked with Randy because he could handle himself, not just because he was with Boyd.

But Randy still burned with vengeful wrath at those who had tortured him before his becoming. And Willem was definitely on that list. I saw Randy immediately head for his room, and I imagined him digging out duct tape and zip ties and his favorite large knives for an evening of bloody festivities.

"Oh well, what the fuck?" I said.

"Should be interesting at least."

Boyd glanced my way as he was welcoming the new guests. Ivan greeted us all and headed for the kitchen table where he did all his work. Boyd ushered Willem over to the Sky Lizard seat and offered him a beer.

"Don't mind if I do, don't mind if I do. I figured y'all would be having a good time over here, that's why I gave old Ivan a ride. That's what I said, right Ivan, a good time, heh, heh."

Ivan mumbled something unintelligible from the kitchen, neither confirming or denying the veracity of Willem's account.

"Ivan said y'all was keeping that whore Katie over here? That's a good piece of ass, boys, but y'all know that already don't you, heh, heh, heh. I remember her from when her brother first started bringing her to the 4-wheeler parties in Frakes. Pretty little thing back then, probably 10 or so. Nice little pussy, buddy. Ten dollars is all he'd charge for a go on her, heh, heh."

I saw Randy in the doorway of his room, face curled into a murderous and evil grin and I could see he had his machete. Fuck, this was going to get messy. Boyd gave him a slight nod, but holding up his hand, said,

"Now hold on there a minute, Willem. Are you talking about the same person? I don't think you should be talking that way about my friend. You're in my home and I don't appreciate it. Now why don't you hit this joint, and think about how you want to proceed."

Ivan called from the kitchen,

"Boyd, I still need about an hour in here, so if we could not do whatever you have in mind right now. Please?"

"Take it easy, take it easy, nobody's getting hurt out here. Right Willem?" Boyd was speaking in sugary sweetness, but his face was all venom. Willem had turned white, realizing he had made a colossal fuckup. He thought he was going to have some fun talking about a little girl he abused as a child, and instead had insulted his hosts. And we were, in fact, crazy people.

The walls of the Waiting Room felt awfully close to ole Willem as he looked to me for guidance, his eyes pleading for some sort of intervention.

I cleared my throat.

"Not a chance," I said.

There was no way to help him, once the rage got going, I knew that. No reason to fill him with false hope.

"I...I...I...I didn't mean nothing, I was just joking around. Shit man, I didn't know you was tight like that, I'm sorry," Willem backtracked, talking fast, fear choking him as he tried to figure a way out of this. He started to rise, and Randy was there with a firm hand on his shoulder.

"No, no, no, sit. Stay a while. We're all friends here. Just relax," Randy said with icy calmness. "Smoke the weed, man, and chill the fuck out."

Willem started to protest, and I pulled my pistol, cocking the hammer in one smooth motion as it came out.

"We insist," I said with a smile.

"Fuck," I heard Ivan say from the kitchen.

This was not how Willem had envisioned his morning, and it was apparent on his face. You could see the hamster wheel working furiously in his brain as he tried to weigh his options. Eventually, the hamster gave out, and Willem sat back down into the warm embrace of the Sky Lizard's couch. I put my gun back in the holster, figuring the Lizard had Willem in his sights anyway.

"Now then, where are we with this joint, Willem?" Boyd asked politely, lighting it and handing it to him.

"Well, I don't really smoke this stuff that much. But since you insist..." Willem forlornly took the joint and began to puff on it. Boyd picked up his guitar and started to play the Sky Lizard Anthem quietly in the background as he worked to bring Willem into the Waiting Room's grip.

"So, what have you got planned now that you're graduated, Willem?" Willem had concluded his senior year as the all-time leading tackler for the Bobcats. Received zero offers from colleges, though, not even the rinky dink ones. Hard to get seen up there.

Willem was loosening up as the marijuana coursed through his body. "I don't know Boyd; I just don't know. I thought I was gonna have a job lined out with Eli, his daddy owns that Blue River Construction, you know. But it isn't going to work out."

Randy had taken up a position in the hallway, blocking the only exit from the living room. Ivan was still banging away on his computers in the kitchen, though it sounded like he was working much faster now. It wouldn't matter. He couldn't leave until the Room was done either.

Katie was noticeably absent. Little Bro and DooWop had gone to the skate park to look for girls and no one else had stopped by. It was a quiet little setting in the Waiting Room, with only Boyd and me in the living room with Willem as the Room began to have its effect.

"I think Eli's mad at me, boys, he's really taken a hard stance against me, heh, heh," he began. Boyd gave me a sideways glance as he cut back into the chorus. It was a catchy tune, the Sky Lizard Anthem, and seemed to be helping Willem open up about his problems.

"Yeah, he's gotten upset with me, and I never meant for that to happen. You see, boys, I always used to pick on Eli, kind of like I done to Randy there, but probably worse. Anyway, I'm past all that kid's stuff, so I started bringing little Eli with me to hang out more. He's a good little drinker, heh, heh. Likes Vodka and all them fruity kind of drinks you can make out of Vodka."

Ivan leaned in from the kitchen, so he could

catch my eye, with an odd look on his face. He nodded toward Willem, as if to say, "now listen to this next part motherfucker."

I started to wonder if Ivan had actually needed a ride that day, or if he had some other reason for bringing Willem here.

Willem hit the joint and continued,

"We've really become best friends here lately. I have him over to the house all the time, he spends the night and everything. He gets too drunk to drive, you understand." At this Willem looked up at me and Boyd, a wise expression on his face.

"Friends don't let friends drive drunk, so I take his keys from him."

He nodded to himself, content in the knowledge that he was in fact a good friend to Eli, despite what Eli might tell him during this current tiff. Willem was looking off into the distance now, eyes glassy and voice taking on a detached somber tone.

"He gets drunk, and I take his keys, and sometimes he wants to wrestle me to get them back. But he's no match for me, I'm much too big. So, once he wears himself out, I put him in the bed, take his shoes off and his jeans, heh, heh. He just lays there, looks like an angel when he sleeps."

Randy was staring at us from the hallway, a look of shock and awe on his face. He raised his machete slightly and nodded toward Willem. Boyd paused the Anthem long enough to slightly shake his head at Randy, and say,

"Please continue, Willem."

I was glad, because I couldn't resist wanting to see where this was going.

"Well, anyways, sometimes when he's lying there, passed out, he looks so cute and sweet, I just crawl in there with him. I get to thinking about us wrestling and I just can't help myself, I roll him over, slip his shorts down and fuck him, nice and slow. He seems to like it slow. Sometimes he'll start to wake up, and I just whisper in his ear, it's just a bad dream babe, just a bad dream, and he just falls back asleep."

"So, what do you see as the problem, Willem? Why do you say he's mad at you?" I asked, genuinely curious if he was going to say the raping, or if he had some other reason he thought Eli was mad at him.

"I think he woke up all the way the other night,

and now he's mad about it. I told him we made this love hundreds of times, but he's still upset. Won't even talk to me and definitely won't come over. And his daddy said he wasn't going to hire me this summer."

Ivan had stopped working on his computers and was standing in the kitchen doorway, staring at Willem, in disbelief that he had actually just told us all that shit.

"It's like a bad dream," Willem mumbled, eyes closed as he soaked in the pot buzz. This was some of Betty's formaldehyde weed, so he was pretty fucked up, I'm sure. One of Betty's nephews was always soaking his brown frown funk in formaldehyde to try and make it better. It definitely made it crazier, although I wasn't sure if it was making it better.

Katie emerged from Randy's room. She had returned from wherever she had been and entered through Randy's window. Or I suppose she could have been there the whole time. In any case, she passed through the living room and into the kitchen without announcement.

That didn't alarm me, since she was Mute Katie, she always walked around without announcement.

But the look on her face made me nervous, so I followed her into the kitchen, calling out behind me,

"Gonna grab a beer, anybody want one?"

I found Katie in the corner, crushing up oxy on the counter and dumping it into a beer she had poured into a glass.

"Whatcha dooooooin?" I asked nonjudgmentally.

"I'm gonna kill him.," she said simply. "Don't worry, not here. This will knock him out and then I'll take him somewhere and kill him."

She looked up from crushing another few pills.

"You can help if you want."

This was just about the most I had ever hear her speak at one time. She had a nice sounding voice, even if she was conspiring to commit a murder.

Ivan had returned to the kitchen table, although he wasn't doing too much working on his computers. He looked disturbed and concerned, but he did say,

"She's not wrong."

I agreed, she wasn't wrong. And she knew a lot more about Willem than me, it seemed. So, I helped her crush up a couple more oxy's, stir them into the beer, and I brought it on out to Willem.

He barely opened his eyes as he took the drugged beer from my hand.

Katie had followed me out of the kitchen and perched on the arm of the Sky Lizard Couch, staring intently at Willem as he chugged the beer, leaned back into the Sky Lizard's .45 and passed out.

After a few minutes of intense staring, Katie said,

"He's ready."

"Ready for what," Randy asked.

"Yes, what indeed." Boyd said. "What was in that beer?"

"Six oxy's or so, as far as I could tell," I said, looking to Katie for clarification. She merely shrugged, her eyes never leaving Willem.

"You want to kill him?" Boyd asked the Room.

"No!" Ivan hollered from the kitchen. I wondered why he had brought Willem here, if he had an idea what was going on with Willem and Eli.

Maybe he thought we would beat Willem up. Or notify the authorities. If Ivan really knew us, he would have known the authorities were never an option.

Randy shrugged. Katie nodded emphatically in the affirmative. Willem snored peacefully.

But I knew Boyd wasn't really asking us. The Waiting Room called the shots.

At that moment, Little Bro and DooWop popped in with a shout, "Honeys, we're home!"

"Who's this motherfucker?" DooWop asked as he dance stepped across the room and flipped on the stereo. Beck's "Fuckin With My Head" flooded the room. I lit a joint, cause the Room was fucking with my head. I passed it to Boyd, who was still waiting for clarification.

"He's a rapist," Ivan called from the kitchen, unable to remain quiet.

Little Bro looked to Randy for confirmation, who nodded his head, and said,

"Rapes little girls and boys."

Little Bro, every day of 11 years old, produced a joint from his cigarette pack, stuck it in his mouth, lit it, and said,

"Well, shoot him in the dick then."

He passed his joint to Katie, who took it with a smile and began nodding enthusiastically.

I felt a smile spreading across my face, a smile that matched the grin on Boyd's face.

"All right, it's settled then," he said.

"Jacko pull Willem's car around, and Randy help me get him out of here."

Little Bro and DooWop helped Boyd and Randy get set up, with Willem between them, one leg tied to each of theirs. It was sort of like a double three-legged race, with each of them moving one of his legs with their own, and his arms around each of their necks, while they held tightly to each hand. It was an awkward way to move a body, but with a hat on the incapacitated person, Boyd and Randy just looked like two guys helping their drunk friend down the stairs.

Not that we moved a lot of bodies, you understand. At least not in one piece.

We drove him out to the edge of town, to a little closed down gas station that still had a pay phone. We parked him next to the phone, moved him into the driver's seat, and Little Bro dialed 911.

"Help, they've shot him in the dick!" he yelled into the receiver, and left the receiver dangling, with the 911 operator asking for more information about his emergency.

She got all the information she was going to get as Katie shot Willem at point blank range twice in the dick. She had a mask on, just in case he woke up from the trauma, but he barely flinched. She might have gone overboard on the pill dosage, but it was too late to worry about that as we sped off into the night.

We heard about it the next day, Betty telling us about how they found some drunk bastard with his dick shot off over by the abandoned Exxon.

"Motherfuckers that have that kind of shit happen to them, there's a reason. Probably raped somebody or something like that," she concluded. We all agreed with her that a lot of the time, people that got their dick shot off probably deserved it.

That night, as I headed off to bed, Katie stopped me in the hall. She threw her arms around me, hugged me tight, and whispered,

"Thank you."

Willem was in a coma for 8 days, and when he finally came to, he couldn't remember anything. The doctors said he had so much oxycontin in his system he should have been dead. And they said he lost so much blood from being shot in the dick that he should have died. They were surprised as shit when he woke up.

He was making the rounds, a couple months after his miraculous recovery, when he stopped by the Waiting Room to tell us the good news.

"Have you heard the Good News?" he asked as soon as he sat down.

"Your dick grew back?" Little Bro asked. Laughing, DooWop punched him in the arm.

"You can't break his balls like that!" he said, grinning from ear to ear.

"At least not anymore!" DooWop spat out between horse laughs. The laugh got the better of him, at which point he fell off the armrest of the love seat and lay in the floor cackling. Little Bro and DooWop were not about to give Willem a pass on anything. He was still a piece of shit, in their opinions, and they were cutting him no slack.

"No, no, of course not," Willem said matter of factly. "I mean, have you heard the Good News about Jesus?"

Katie shook her head at DooWop and Little Bro, who had joined his compatriot in cackling on the floor at Jesus. Boyd nodded to Willem, and said,

"While some of the uninitiated here have no idea what you're talking about, some of us are familiar. Hell, Randy and Jack are practically experts, having grown up the sons of preacher men."

"Well, Boys, I'm here to tell you that I've been saved. I went through that light in the tunnel and on the other side, God in his Glory told me I was forgiven, and that I was going back to tell others. And here I am! Now I done some awful, unspeakable things, with my dick over the years, and that's why God took it from me. It's so I can be a better Christian brother to all the rest of you." He paused for dramatic effect, and concluded,

"I tell you what, Boys, waking up with no dick was the best day of my life. I'm free to be the Good Lord's messenger!"

And with that, he passed out pamphlets to each one of us, even those who were clearly unbelievers, inviting us to the revival they were having over in Harrogate at the Tex Turner Arena next weekend. Willem was the featured speaker, according to the pamphlet.

Well, except for God of course, who would be speaking to each of us in our hearts, according to the pamphlet. As he handed each of us a pamphlet, he hugged us, working his way around the room, thanking us for letting him talk to us and telling us he was praying for us and would we please pray for him too.

As Boyd double locked the door behind him, I let out a sigh of relief.

"What the fuck was that?" Randy asked.

"I think it means we're in the clear, cause that motherfucker clearly doesn't know what in the fuck happened to him," Boyd answered.

"And I think it might mean we work for God?" I asked, only half joking. We were all well aware that Karma did not have fists, so sometimes humans had to use their fists to beat somebody's ass that Karmically needed an ass beating.

It stood to reason that God might also need a human to shoot a guy's dick off now and then to accomplish His goals.

"The Lord works in mysterious ways, his wonders to perform," Little Bro said in a soft, hallowed voice. He almost pulled it off, but a smirk started to creep into the corners of his mouth, and then DooWop laughed, and then Katie, and then all the rest of us too.

"To doing the Lord's work!" Boyd said, heading to the kitchen for a round of beers.

Randy already had the pamphlets all gathered

up in the ashtray and was lighting them on fire by the time Boyd got there with the beers.

"I guess we aren't going," I mumbled, opening my beer and taking a swig.

As I drank my beer, laughing with the rest, I wondered what Jesus would have said, about us working for him and all.

Could have asked him, I guess, if his face wasn't covered by the High Voltage sticker.

Ten

Freebird

By this point, DooWop was running a very successful card game out of the Waiting Room, which was a welcome change of pace. We hadn't had much organized entertainment since Bubbles, Ivan, and Bobby had come over to resurrect their old school Dungeons and Dragons game they used to do with Boyd and Randy. They made me play, even though I didn't want to, and they eventually came around to appreciate my sentiment.

The problem was that we were smoking that damn formaldehyde weed from Betty's nephew again, and I got way too into the game. I thought Boyd wanted me to kill Bobby in real life, not just in the game, and the Sky Lizard was definitely egging the whole thing on. They sent me to my room, and Katie filled in, although it was hard because she didn't talk.

Ever since then, the idea of organized gaming had been a little taboo in the Waiting Room. But DooWop changed all that. He liked dealing Blackjack, but he would deal poker too, and he and Little Bro came up with some poker chips and started a regular game on Wednesday nights. They would move the kitchen table out into the living room, set up the chairs around it, sell and cash the chips and keep 10% of every pot. They kept it simple, with $100 caps on the betting and it was a great way to spend an evening. We would sit around, smoking dope and drinking beer and cheering on the participants who seemed to feel like they were just a step below the World Series of Poker. At least that's how it looked from my vantage point on the couch.

All sorts passed through, but a semi-regular group emerged. FreeBird was the most successful player out of the regulars. FreeBird had honed his skills at the Bell County Detention Center over the course of many months serving time over the years for a variety of societal sins. Most often, he was busted on drunk and disorderly, and he had a bad habit of punching cops. So, he'd end up with a few months here, a few months there, and eventually he turned himself into a pretty good card player.

I had met FreeBird several years back, when I was still running with Jimmy and Walter and the Pineville potheads I met when I first moved into the area. Potheads are some of the easiest kids to get to know. Just bring pot and you're in. On the day I met FreeBird, Jimmy and I were headed to the mall so he could get a present for his girlfriend's birthday. FreeBird ended up tagging along.

"Let's stop and get some beer," he said as soon as he got into the car. "I brung this good Jim Beam," he said, although Jim Beam is rarely good and the bottle was mostly drank already. We swung out by the bootlegger anyway, although I was determined not to drink too much until I was away from the mall and the mall cops.

Mall cops are not really anything to worry about, they can't really arrest you. They can call the real cops though, so you do have to keep from being caught by them. Which is really not that hard. No Mall Cop actually wants to chase you. They would rather mosey around the food court eating cookies and looking at girls. The occasional shoplifter from the record store is about all the criminality the Mall Cop wants to handle.

They were not prepared for FreeBird post-Jim Beam. Jimmy and I thought we were in the clear when we arrived at the mall, because FreeBird had passed out in the back of the car. We left him there while Jimmy went to look for a present and I went to hit on this girl I knew at the movie theatre. She sold tickets at the box office and I had the hots for her, which had caused me to buy far too many tickets for movies I never wanted to see. This was early on, before my drug habits consumed all the discretionary funds.

I got back to the parking lot, with a ticket for some Nicholas Cage film I would never see, and found a crowd had formed near my car. I pushed my way through the cheering and raucous spectators so I could see what all the fuss was about.

To my dismay, I discovered that FreeBird was awake, he was out of the car, and he was beating the hell out of two Mall cops. I wasn't sure what to do, exactly, still being fairly new to the country, but luckily Jimmy appeared at my elbow and said,

"Stay back, man. The real cops are here and there's no need us all getting arrested and your car impounded." I realized he was right, as the blue lights and screaming sirens filled the air. Only one Mall Cop seemed able to hear it, though, because I am pretty sure the fat one was unconscious. The skinny one was backpedaling in a circle, trying to stay out of FreeBird's range until the police arrived. He was successful, but as the MPD arrived on the scene, the first one to reach for FreeBird got a fistful of rage to his eye.

Jimmy let out a whoop and a holler and a "Get 'em FreeBird!" which started a cheer among the bystanders. Nobody really likes cops anyway, and FreeBird had just decked one. The second cop was already on to the taser though, which took some time to really work. The skinny Mall Cop tried to get in there too quickly and got tased too, which made us all laugh, even FreeBird as he was convulsing on the ground. They finally managed to get him in the police car, to the onlookers' chants of "FreeBird, FreeBird, FreeBird!"

"Don't worry," Jimmy said. "Happens almost every time I bring him to the mall. We'll go see him in the jail tomorrow, bring him some cigarettes."

"Why do you bring him, if he's just going to fight a Mall Cop and get arrested?" I asked.

"It's a free country," Jimmy said simply. "Gotta let people live their life."

The next time I saw FreeBird was at Jimmy's father's funeral. Jimmy, Sr. had not been well loved by most of us. My few encounters with him had been slightly hostile and needlessly rude, in my opinion. And the scuttlebutt was that he was a terrible brute to Jimmy's mother, Savannah. Jimmy never said his dad ever beat him or anything, but Savannah broke it down for me a week or so after the funeral. She always liked to talk to me when I'd come over to smoke weed with Jimmy. She would make me come into the living room, sit down with her and smoke a couple of cigarettes while she unburdened her soul. Or at least that's what it felt like was going on.

"Jack, it's like this," she was telling me, that night not long after the funeral. "My husband was an asshole. He beat me for years, anytime I ever even disagreed about anything. Or didn't have supper ready in time. Or wanted money for a new dress. Or shoes for the boy. My husband was a mean old son of a bitch."

She slowly raised her Virginia Slim in its silver holder to her lips and took a long slow draw. Every movement of her smoking was in deliberate slow motion. Had to be that way, since she never ashed her cigarettes. She would have a damn three-inch-long ash on the end of that thing, and still sit there smoking it. It was fascinating to watch while you were stoned, to see if this would be the moment that the ash tumbled from the end and made a mess down the front of her shirt.

But it was never the moment.

Savannah continued, "So when he said he was finally going to kill me, I believed him. He had that look." I wasn't sure what that look was, having never known anyone before who was actually going to kill someone. I smoked my cigarette in silence, and waited for her to go on.

"I took that .357 from the bedside table and stuck in my back pocket, under my sweater where he couldn't see it and went on about my day. He had gone to town to get some cigarettes. And when he came through that door, cussing and talking crazy, I pulled and emptied it in him." She exhaled slowly. "I say he came at me, of course, but I was going to defend myself either way. He was going to kill me, or hurt my little Jimmy, and I couldn't let that happen. It was the only way we could be safe. And I'll do it again in a New York minute to anybody that tries to hurt me or my boy."

She nodded decisively, assured that she had made the right choice and pulled another Virginia Slim from her pack inside her little black leather case. She had a case or a holder for everything and I marveled that she hadn't had a holster for the gun and had just put it in her back pocket like a commoner; but I didn't say anything about that.

Instead, I said,

"You gotta do what you gotta do to protect your loved ones, I guess."

"Damn straight," she said as she turkey fucked her new cigarette off the old one, having finally knocked the full-length ash into the ashtray to gain access to the burning ember. She secured the new cigarette in the holder and snubbed out the old butt.

"Damn fucking straight," she repeated.

Things got weird with Jimmy after his father died. He really struggled with it, overdosing once behind McDonald's and almost dying. Bubbles found him and called 911. Of course, when they got there and found dope on Bubbles, he said it was Jimmy's since Jimmy was incapacitated and might die anyway. Bubbles was kind of a douche.

And after I transferred schools, I didn't run with that crowd as much. So, when FreeBird showed up for DooWop's card game it was a welcome reunion of sorts. He had cut down significantly on his drinking, he said, producing a half pint bottle from his pocket instead of the fifth bottle he normally packed around with him.

"I ain't punched a cop in six months," he explained. "But you know Jimmy, he's still drinking heavy. It's a wonder he hasn't run that pretty little girlfriend of his off, bless her heart. Not many would put up with a drunk like that."

I agreed Charlotte was a gem, but I didn't really want to get too involved in a conversation about Jimmy. You see, Boyd had a very low opinion of Savannah. He said it was because he didn't buy her self-defense story that had gotten her off with the cops. He thought it was more premeditated and sort of in cold blood.

I knew there was another reason Boyd didn't like Savannah though, they had a history. Even though he had not seen it firsthand, I knew Free-Bird knew the reason too, which was why he was content to drop the discussion of Jimmy and his family and focus on playing cards. And you had to focus in that room, or DooWop would take all your damn money.

Concentrating on his cards, FreeBird finally asked for our help. It wasn't for him, you understand, that would have been easy although unlikely because FreeBird rarely needed help with anything. At least not with something like this.

Jimmy had a problem. His girl. She was the problem, although Jimmy wasn't ready to see it that way. She had stepped out on him, which was nothing new. The girl practically lived outside, she stepped out on him so much. Everybody knew that this was the case, but everybody also backed off from Jimmy after his dad died.

I'm sure nobody meant for it to be that way. I know I convinced myself that it was because I switched schools. I don't know what others convinced themselves of. The fact remained, the girl-friend was a whore and nobody wanted to be the one to tell Jimmy.

Not even FreeBird, who was his best friend.

"Look Boys, it's like this here: I know she's a slut. You know she's a slut. But Jimmy Boy loves her and wants to protect her and wants to beat the tar out of this motherfucker that's fucked her lately," he explained to us while DooWop was dealing Texas Hold 'Em.

I wasn't playing, mostly because I suck at cards. And I didn't have any money to lose in the money game. I would play in the smokes game, for cigarettes. I could always get more cigarettes. But hard currency was usually hard to come by, and defi-nitely hard to hold on to. DooWop's cash game was not geared toward us who lived there, it was meant to take the guests' money.

"And here's the problem. This guy knows he fucked up, and is ducking our boy Jimmy. I'm in for $2, DooWop," FreeBird said, eyeing his hole cards.

Ivan put himself in, as did Bubbles. Randy folded, which was always the best thing he could do in a hand. Randy was the only person I ever even had a shot of beating in a card game. And even that was rare.

FreeBird continued,

"The little dick motherfucker is hiding. And Jimmy ain't allowed to leave his domicile on account of he's on house arrest and all, over cracking that douchebag's skull that fucked his old lady the last time, you remember."

FreeBird watched the flop materialize as DooWop put down a 10 of spades, then a Jack and another 10, both diamonds. FreeBird let out a whistle, muttering, "deal 'em, brother," under his breath.

"I'll go another $2, DooWop," he said.

We did remember, at least I did. I had seen it. Jimmy *had* cracked that dude's skull with a brick.

Of course, there were no witnesses who would say that was what had happened. But we all saw Jerry, who had fucked Jimmy's girl at the party the night before, hit Jimmy over the head with a beer bottle in the midst of their scuffle that next morning. And we saw Jimmy swing a brick he picked up from beside the patio wall into the side of Jerry's head as Jerry came in at him with the broken bottle.

Jerry was down, and twitching in the driveway when I split. FreeBird had stayed to talk to the cops with Jimmy and the girlfriend. I don't think the judge totally believed their story about Jerry just flipping out and coming at Jimmy with a broken bottle and it all being self-defense, because Jimmy did get the house arrest. But nobody else was ever questioned about it and nobody came forward with any other information.

In a cosmic sense, I guess you shouldn't fuck other people's girlfriends.

Ivan folded, but Bubbles and DooWop both ponied up, with Bubbles raising $3 more. DooWop thought about it for a minute, then put his $3 in too.

"I'll go three more, let's see that turn, boys," FreeBird said, which wasn't the greatest segue into what he said next.

"I need you boys to bring this bastard that's lately been fucking Jimmy's old lady to Jimmy and me, so we can take care of things. He won't ride in a car with me."

DooWop flipped over the turn, a 7 of spades. Bubbles checked, as did DooWop.

"Now it gets interesting with that 7," FreeBird said. He added,

"I'll go $5 more, boys."

"You're trying to buy your way out of it now, motherfucker, and I'm gonna let you," Bubbles said, leaning his giant frame back in his chair, clearly annoyed with himself for not having the stones to see if what he said was true.

"That... is interesting," Boyd said, picking up his guitar.

"It's mighty Jimmygerous down there at Jimmy's, excitable folks around and all. I don't think I'm welcome down there with Savannah." He began to play the Sky Lizard's anthem, at about half the usual tempo. Sort of slow and groovy.

DooWop was studying his hole cards and contemplating the size of his stones in relation to Bubbles, who had folded, while slowly nodding along with Boyd's playing. He looked to be talking himself into it, while FreeBird continued to try to talk us into his operation.

DooWop threw a $5 in and flipped the River card. Queen of Spades.

"And then, of course, there's the Bitch," Free-

Bird said, glancing around the room before continuing,

"I'll tell you what, boys, it'll be worth your while, believe me. I'll go a hundred on this river card right here, like a deposit" he said. He pulled Mr. Franklin from his shirt pocket and placed it in the pile.

DooWop raised his eyebrows and sat back in his chair, looking slowly from the pile of money, to his hole cards, to Randy, then to me, then to Boyd.

Boyd stopped playing in mid strum, and said,

"I can take that action, but it will have to be $500, FreeBird, on account of the Bitch being around there."

FreeBird sat back in his chair, took off his cap and scratched his balding head. Male pattern baldness strikes early in the mountains sometimes. Probably the mine runoff in the water.

"I can go $200 now," FreeBird said, placing another hundred in the pot. "And another $100 when you show up with the prize. And I fold this shitty hand, for now," he said, pushing his cards into the middle.

Boyd nodded and started playing the anthem

again, while DooWop scooped up our money. We were hired.

As FreeBird got up to leave, he said,

"Jack, I'll trust you to make sure this goes smooth, brother." I nodded my consent, although I knew shit was rarely ever going to go smoothly.

"Who's the mark?" I asked, figuring proper identification would probably help.

"Y'all know him. Tobey Wayne Miracle. Send word on the details, so we'll be ready," he called as he headed out of the Waiting Room, his task and his time completed.

I shook my head, Tobey Wayne fucking Miracle. Little shithead was always talking shit and trying to be a hardass. He drove a classic old school 1968 Mustang that he had fixed up at his uncle's mechanic shop. His uncle had been fixing it up to sell, but Tobey Wayne whined so much about it that his Daddy bought it for him at cost.

It was far too fine an automobile for this type of douchebag. As I had heard it said, he couldn't even change the oil in the thing. According to PorkChop, who sometimes passed through for a beer and a joint on his way home from work at the uncle's garage,

"The little bastard is just so fucking entitled. Doesn't want to get his hands dirty and won't learn the simplest things to help out. Just bitches about the music and his clothes getting dirty and how the grease won't come off his hands. I told him to quit forgetting his fucking gloves as a good start."

I always liked PorkChop, he'd tell it how it is.

And Little Bro had had a run in with the little prince as well, walking home from school one day. Tobey had splashed him with a giant mud puddle, gunning the engine in the Mustang and swerving over to plow through the puddle, sending a watery arc of nastiness raining down on Little Bro.

Naturally, Little Bro had thrown a rock at him in retaliation, and Tobey Wayne had shot him up with a paintball gun before speeding off in his shiny toy. Tobey's daddy owned a local oil distribution company, small time in the grand scheme of things, but for that neck of the woods they were big shots.

So, Tobey Wayne Miracle was a rich little prick who we already didn't like. And now he was going to get beat for screwing somebody's old lady. I figured with a mark like that, this operation could only go smoothly.

Eleven

Shit's Never Smooth

Ever the voice of reason, Boyd brought my positive thinking down a notch after Bubbles and Ivan left.

"I don't know about this, fellas, that Savanah is crazier than a pet monkey," he said, continuing, "It will be really hard not to shoot her and claim self-defense. Especially if we play it like Tobey Wayne is our friend and her, Jimmy, and FreeBird are attacking us. We could do all three and the cops would totally buy it. She's fucking batshit and they all know it. Be doing society a favor if you think about it."

"But who's gonna believe Tobey Wayne is our friend?" Little Bro asked. There were murmurs of consent and nodding heads around the room.

Katie was wholeheartedly onboard for fragging Tobey Wayne, at least as indicated by her emphatic nodding. And Randy was thinking about it, I could tell, despite Little Bro's very valid point. I figured this might have been what FreeBird was talking about, when he said to make it go smoothly.

Boyd definitely had it in for Savanah, going on a couple of years now.

Boyd had gone over to Jimmy's for a party one night, flying solo. I was trying to shag some girl from school, and Randy was still staying with his Dad. So, Boyd went on his own, unarmed, which might have been a mistake.

He had gotten way too drunk, as is usually the goal at somebody else's party, and passed out in one of the bedrooms. Apparently, some of the party guests had decided it would be funny to draw on him with lipstick and makeup and a sharpie while he was passed out.

Boyd woke up with bright red lips and dark blue eyeshadow and a cock drawn on his cheek and 'skull fuck' written on his forehead. He flipped out, of course, and threatened to kill several of the girls who woke up to his cursing and screaming. He promptly knocked Jimmy out, one punch, when he had come busting out of his room like he wanted some.

I don't know what Boyd was planning to do to Jimmy, unconscious on the floor, because he never got the chance. As Boyd stood over her boy, Savanah, who had just emerged from her bedroom, brought the sites on her trusty revolver to bear on Boyd's chest, center mass, and said,

"You better step away from my son you painted up bastard, or this is the last sound you'll ever hear!" And she cocked back the hammer.

Boyd put his hands up, left without a word, walked down to the river to wash his face off as best he could, and followed the river down to where it met the train tracks and followed the tracks back home. He was still living with his parents, and luckily Hippy John was out. Big Carolyn cleaned him up and tried to convince him not to go back with a shotgun and kill the whole houseful of 'em.

Which she successfully did, for that day. He wouldn't want her to know if he did do it, wouldn't want her to perjure herself. Boyd still seethed with anger, and had concocted several different plans to knock Savanah off. We generally were able to stave off these maniacal bouts of psychosis with a proper dosage of barbiturates and opiates.

And pot helped.

In all honesty, I wasn't entirely on board with killing Savanah anyway. She had been defending her son, after all. It has still never been established if Jimmy had anything to do with drawing on Boyd or not. And I kind of liked Savanah. It was probably my morbid curiosity to a certain extent. She was the first person I knew that killed someone, and the only person I knew who would talk to me about it.

She was sad that she had killed her husband, I think. And I do think she thought it was the only choice she really had. Her husband's family was too entrenched in that town, owning several big businesses. She had never gotten any relief from the court system in regards to him beating the shit out of her, or Jimmy. Small towns are like that sometimes. Big towns too.

So, when she pulled that trigger, I think she was doing all that she knew to do. Emptying it into his lifeless body was probably overboard, but emotions were probably running high at the time. At least she didn't reload.

As for Boyd's beef with her, if he had been armed and shot her in the face, he would have been justified. She pulled a gun on him and he hadn't actually done anything to Jimmy besides defend himself when Jimmy came at him. Legally, he was in their house and all, and was the initial aggressor I suppose, but in my book, when the guns come out, it's kill or be killed. So, I wouldn't have thought any less of him if it had gone that way.

But it didn't go that way, and to come back on her now, after all this time, is very clearly premeditated murder. The heat of the moment is gone, the imminent threat is gone, the self-defense is gone. All that's left is you don't like this person and you want to kill them. Over some lipstick and shit.

"I don't think we need to kill FreeBird," I began the negotiation. "He hasn't done anything."

Boyd lit a cigarette as he considered this possibility. Katie rolled her eyes. Randy shook his head incredulously. DooWop shrugged and went back to working on his dance moves. He was working his way through Michael Jackson's 'dangerous' album. Kid loved Michael Jackson. Little Bro yawned at me, and the Sky Lizard trained his .45 at my head.

Boyd spoke for the room, which happened sometimes,

"Fuck FreeBird. He picked his side long ago."

And that was that. The Waiting Room had spoken. We set about plotting and scheming, and scheming and plotting the demise of my friend, my other friend, and his mother. I realized I did think of Jimmy and FreeBird as my friends, and this murder plot really was getting out of hand.

We settled on Boyd and me accompanying Pavo to find Tobey Wayne and get him fucked up enough to not realize we were pulling up at Jimmy's house. We couldn't bring Randy since Pavo might not want to really hang out with Randy. Randy always made sure to put Pavo in his place in front of new people, which Tobey Wayne would qualify as.

And we needed Pavo to make us look less threatening. People trusted Pavo. He was a smooth-talking motherfucker, and people wanted to buy what he was selling.

But we knew we had to keep Pavo in the dark about the whole thing, really, so we needed to think of a reason to have him bring Tobey Wayne. Pavo was smart enough to figure things out if he knew we were headed there with any kind of agenda. And he absolutely could not keep his mouth shut.

"Now shit should go smooth, because if they are planning to tune this Tobey up, I bet Jimmy and FreeBird won't be packing. We'll bring a couple of throwdowns for after, so Randy, we're gonna need two cheap pieces of shit, untraceable to us, and wiped clean. We can stage the scene while Pavo comforts Tobey in the car. Jesus, we should bring tissue but that will look premeditated. I bet Pavo will have Kleenex in his car anyway, whimpering fuck that he is." Boyd outlined the plan with cold precision.

If Pavo really didn't know anything about it beforehand he would be an invaluable witness with the cops. He was a silver-tonged motherfucker, and people liked to believe him.

Plus, we knew he would be freaked out by Jimmy and FreeBird seemingly attacking us, and his traumatically heartfelt testimony to our self-defense plea would work wonders on the cops. Between him and Tobey Wayne gushing over the heroical nature of our defending them from the attackers, we figured we'd be in the clear.

At least that's how Boyd was explaining it, to the rapt attention of all us co-conspirators.

I felt detached as I nodded along, and mumbled my consent. It didn't feel right, talking out how to kill Jimmy and FreeBird. I really liked those guys. But you don't always feel like you get to choose. Sometimes you're in a place where there just don't seem to be any options, and once you're started down a path you don't see anything else to do but empty the gun in him.

It was Betty that snapped me out of it. I was headed to the bodega the next morning to get some smokes when she called for me to wait up.

"Slow down, I gotta talk to you," she hissed as she came up, walking quickly.

"Go down the alley a ways."

When we were halfway down the alley, in the stretch by the dumpsters where there weren't any windows, she laid it all out for me.

"I can hear every word you crazy ass mother-fuckers say," she began.

"That's why I keep my TV so loud. Cause I don't wanna know. But last night I was trying this thing with Jefferson where he have to be absolutely silent no matter what I do to him, and anyway, we heard the whole thing about killing FreeWilly and his momma. And you know damn well that blabbermouth Pavo is gonna get you fools busted. He can't keep his mouth shut about shit! And he's smarter than you dumbasses think. Plus, you can't have them innocent children involved! What the fuck is the matter with you?!"

I wasn't sure if she was calling Katie, Little Bro, or DooWop innocent, but regardless of who she meant, I wasn't sure I agreed with her assessment of their character. In any case, if she heard it, then Jefferson heard it too. And God knows who else in the building.

Fucking paper-thin walls.

"Alright listen," I said after a moment. "Don't say anything to Boyd and the others, I don't want

them to know everything you know. But let me figure out how to call the whole thing off. Just don't
let them know you are involved."

"Involved? I'm not involved with you crazy
fuckin' white boys! I'm just letting you know, so
you can take care of it."

And with that she marched on down the alley
and toward the bodega. I walked back to the parking lot and the car, got in, and drove to a pay
phone.

"We need to talk," I said to FreeBird when he
finally answered the phone. He agreed and I drove
over to meet up with him and Jimmy.

I knew I needed to broach the subject gently, so
as not to spook them and make matters worse.

"We've got a major fucking problem," I said as I
got out of the car, contrary to my own advice. We
had met at the State Park, which was a great place
to meet somebody and talk out of earshot of anyone.

Unless it was tourist season, they all said when
I moved to the mountains. Except I had been there
six years and had yet to see a tourist. Maybe they'll
be back next season.

"What do you mean?" Jimmy asked. "FreeBird

already gave you more money than he should have. What's the problem?" FreeBird nodded, apparently agreeing that he had in fact overpaid.

"Let me back up," I said, trying to find the words to convey catastrophe, but in a calming and soothing kind of way. The humans are hard to talk to, and I had apparently not smoked enough pot to calm my anxiety.

"I feel that this whole thing would go better if Savanah and Boyd weren't coming together in such a way. I feel like life has been pretty good for all of us with them staying away from each other," I said calmly.

"Aw, shit!" FreeBird said as he spat. "they ain't neither one gonna do nothing. But if you feel that way, just leave Boyd out of it. Y'all got paid either way."

"Well, I thought of that, thought of bringing Randy instead. But I need Pavo to get Tobey Wayne, and Pavo and Randy don't get along, and Boyd is way better to have in that type of situation anyway. So, I was hoping we could try to schedule it when Savanah is out of town or something," I said, hoping they would see it my way.

"Boyd is the problem, not my mom," Jimmy

said defensively. "I don't think we should have to worry about whether he is going to start some shit or not. You're doing a job for us."

"While I concede that Boyd is a hothead, I think we can all agree that Savanah can fly off the handle at times too. I don't think any of us would honestly be surprised if she was the one that started talking shit to him," I said.

FreeBird's face said I had gone too far, given the circumstances surrounding Jimmy Sr.'s untimely demise, but Jimmy let out a sigh. Then he walked over and extended his hand and then pulled me in to give me a hug.

"That's what I love about you, Jacky, you're never afraid to speak your mind. Even if that is a fucked-up thing to say to a guy whose mom shot his dad," and he burst out laughing, followed by FreeBird, and then by me, until we were all laughing at ...I'm not sure what.

But at least we were all on the same page. They agreed to get Savanah out of the house for the weekend, send her to visit her sister for a couple of days, and then let me know when she was gone. We smoked a couple of joints up on the mountain in the state park, watching the sun fade behind the hills and plunge the hollers into darkness, talking about how the tourism industry had dried up like the rest of the industries, but fuck it, cause the mountains sure are beautiful in the right light, and tourists suck anyway.

I felt a little duplicitous when I finally made it back to the Waiting Room, with a lame excuse about going to see my parents. Randy bought it, but not Boyd. He never did ask about it though. I had sold us out, but I knew it had to be done.

I heard from FreeBird that we were on for Saturday night, and we set about gathering up Pavo and Tobey Wayne. It was DooWop who came up with the plan to get those two clowns together.

"Why don't we just tell Pavo that Katie has a thing for Tobey and ask him to bring him over for her birthday party. We'll get him fucked up, then you go on a beer run or something and, disco," he said. Katie was shaking her head violently, which prompted Randy to say,

"But Katie doesn't have a thing for Tobey, and that puts her in an awkward spot all night, having to pretend she is into this douchebag."

"It's not her birthday either," DooWop said, "but she still gets to have a party."

Katie brightened up at the thought of throwing herself a party, even if she had to keep a douchebag at bay, and DooWop's plan was adopted.

Luckily, Katie knew how to organize a party. She made lists of instructions for each of us, party supplies to acquire, guests to invite, drugs to procure. She also organized the cleaning and the straightening up, such as it was.

She organized through post it notes, which really brightened up the place as she stuck little notes with each of our names on them and precise party prep instructions all over the Waiting Room.

Boyd was a firm believer in clutter as part of the ambiance, so she had to fight him tooth and nail the whole time, which made for some great entertainment for the rest of us, as she would put things away and he would rescue them from the closet or the cupboard or the shelf and return them to their places of prominence on the coffee table, end table, and corner pile.

Randy made a giant Happy Birthday banner that stretched across the room, hung over the Lord's Supper with a little help from Little Bro, who was himself hungover. Even Betty got in on the birthday action, making Jefferson BBQ a pork shoulder for pulled pork sandwiches. She also whipped up some amazing potato salad.

Margot came by and baked a cake, the first non-pot infused food we had ever baked in that oven. It turned out to be one hell of a party, and I would have had a really great time if it wasn't all leading up to an absolutely fucked up ending for one of the party guests.

Randy, of course, almost gave it away multiple times while trying to be clever. Luckily, he got too drunk too early and passed out before he could really spill the beans. Katie flirted with Tobey for about a half a second, then ignored him the rest of the night. He didn't seem to mind, being totally enthralled by one of Margot's friends.

Katie did come round to slip some ketamine into his drink at one point and smoke a giant blunt with him and Margot's friend, which put the two of them out. Boyd nodded at me, and we gathered up Pavo, who said he was bored anyway, what with Margot having shot him down for the twentieth time. We loaded Tobey Wayne up in Pavo's ride, telling him we wanted to go get some pot somebody owed us on the way to bringing Tobey

Wayne home. Pavo agreed, and we were on our way.

Pavo didn't catch on to where we were going until we were in World's End, and I was directing him to pass through and onto Four Mile Road.

"Are we going to Jimmy's house?" he asked, adjusting the rearview mirror to see my response from the backseat. I looked out the window.

"Yes, but don't worry about it. Boyd is on his best behavior," I said, reaching up and patting Boyd on the head.

"Fuck you. You know that bitch is crazy. Everybody better watch their ass up here, man. Pavo, make sure you park where we can get away if we need to. You don't know what that fucked up bitch will do," Boyd said as he closed his knife he had been picking at his nails with. He was all nervous energy.

We pulled up, and Pavo swung in wide like an idiot, halfway across the driveway and a little bit in the grass. I wasn't sure what part of "park where we can get away" involved this T-Bone maneuver, but I didn't say anything.

Boyd and I jumped out immediately, which was good, because out of nowhere, Jimmy materialized and was suddenly in the backseat with Tobey Wayne, beating his brains out. FreeBird came out of the house and ran up to Pavo's door and opened it. He reached in and grabbed Pavo and pulled him kicking and screaming out of the door.

I could tell Pavo was hamming it up quite a bit. Pavo was a lover, not a fighter, and he was mostly protesting just in case Tobey was somehow still conscious and could hear him. Pavo had only made a half-hearted effort to restrain Jimmy, from the front seat, and he was happy to be pulled away from the action.

Boyd was still standing by the car, scanning the house. It was completely dark. Ours was the only car in the driveway. I looked over at FreeBird, who had helped Pavo up and was explaining that this was the natural course in the circle of life for ole Tobey. That sometimes, in the wild, one critter will fuck another critter's woman, and sometimes that leads to that first critter getting his ass beat by the second critter, whose wife that first critter had fucked.

It was making sense to me, and I looked over at Boyd, who had his pistol drawn, but held down low by his leg where you wouldn't really notice it in the dark, if you weren't looking for it.

I knew I had to ask, so I said,

"FreeBird, is there anybody else here?"

"Nah," he said, glancing back at me,

"Savanah went to Gatlinburg with her cousin, and Jimmy's old lady is at her mom's for a few days. Till they work some shit out," he said, nodding at Jimmy in the backseat, who was sitting still, for now, having worn himself out with the thrashing. At some point, Tobey Wayne must have opened the door to try to escape, because it was swung all the way open and he was slumped over in the seat, halfway out of the car, unconscious.

Jimmy climbed out of the car, walked around the back, tapping his fingers on the trunk as he went, and slammed the door on Tobey's head and arms with a loud kerchunk.

"Fuck you, motherfucker," he said as he walked back toward the house. I looked at Boyd, who had put his pistol away. I guess with no Savanah, Plan A had become Plan B, which was what we were supposed to have been doing anyway.

"We good?" FreeBird asked as he came over to give me a handshake.

"Yeah, we're good. It was a surprise, but the motherfucker had it coming, I guess. You don't fuck another man's woman," I said with a nod.

"Law of the jungle, Baby," FreeBird said.

"There is the matter of the pot you owe Jacko," Boyd said, a frown on his face. I could tell he was disappointed, but I hoped some pot would help ease the tension.

FreeBird looked confused, so I said,

"Let's you and me go sort that out inside, Free-Bird, and let Pavo and Boyd deal with that one, there."

He nodded and we walked inside. I told him about having told Pavo we were stopping by for some pot, so he and Jimmy broke me off a little $20 bag for my cover, and the remining $80 per the agreement. Under the circumstances I figured that this was about as smooth as this situation was ever going to turn out.

When we got back to the Waiting Room, and relayed the night's events to Katie and Little Bro, who were the only ones still up awaiting news, they seemed disappointed. But a little relieved too. I definitely felt like we had dodged a particularly sticky legal mess. The job hadn't really gone

smoothly, but at least it was over and we could col-
lectively breathe a sigh of relief.

And I could definitely feel Betty's sigh of relief
as well, through the paper-thin walls.

Twelve

Fathead

Fathead used to bring weed by all the time. Nobody exactly liked Fathead all that much on account of you couldn't really trust him. He was a thieving rogue type of asshole, and although he never stole anything from us, as far as we could tell, there was always that suspicion in the back of your mind when he was around. But like I said, he never stole from us. You see, Fathead robbed drug dealers.

He'd gotten pretty good at it over the years, which was surprising. He had an enormous head, like a bobblehead doll. Hence the nickname. And we always figured someday some drug dealer somewhere would realize that this giant headed prick in a double XL ski mask shoving a gun in their face was Fathead. But he hadn't gotten caught so far. It was indeed a mystery.

Of course, not everyone knew that was what he was doing, and we weren't rats, especially not about stuff that came out in the Waiting Room. I think Fathead liked coming over because he knew the Room didn't care who you were or what you'd done. It was a judgement free zone in that way, child molesters and rapists excepted of course.

And he always brought a nice package of whatever weed and various other dope he had most recently stolen, so we didn't mind too much. And he never stole from us, as far as we could tell.

His running mate was Big D. Big D was the best pool player anyone had ever seen, was probably going to go pro as soon as he was old enough to move out of his momma's house. Momma D didn't really approve of the amount of time he spent in pool halls hustling drunks, being as how he was only 16, and she wasn't about to sign off on him going to Vegas for the big tournaments. She was a little over protective since the accident.

Fathead and Big D's older brother Freddy had been best friends since birth. And they were always into one type of shit or another since birth. On Fathead's birthday a couple of years back, they had decided to steal a car to drive into Lexington to try to sneak into the strip clubs. They made Big D stay home, because they figured there was no way they would be able to get him past the bouncer. Instead, they brough two knuckleheads with them, Mark and Maverick.

Everything went according to plan, except they never made it to Lexington. Maverick insisted they get some whiskey for the drive from the bootlegger up in Frakes, and Fathead lost control of the car on that twisting fucking road coming out of the holler and they rolled that stolen/borrowed Beamer down the side of the mountain. Mark was thrown from the car and severed his spinal column at the waist; he would never walk again. Maverick was knocked unconscious and lay in the backseat until the paramedics got there. Big D's brother was pronounced dead at the scene.

Fathead walked away unhurt, like the driver always seems to. The guilt and pain ate at him every day, it looked like, and he never really got over being unhurt when one friend was paralyzed and one friend was dead. He latched onto Big D and tried to be a big brother to him, albeit in his own fucked up Fathead kind of way.

The mom never forgave him, but Big D wasn't so harsh. He knew that if they would have let him go, he would have been right there with them, and if anything, the crash made him more determined than ever not to miss anything ever again. He and Fathead had a tight connection.

At least that's what he said under the influence in front of the Sky Lizard one night when we were discussing the nature of his relationship with Fathead.

"He's gonna get you killed, man," I had said to him. "You've got a talent, man, a real skill that you can use without all this shit Fathead gets you into."

Big D looked up from the pile of cocaine he was carefully mixing with baby laxative and caffeine. He was following Fathead's formula of 1-1-1, which I felt was a shit formula. But I wasn't planning on buying any of it off Fathead anyway.

"Yeah, man," Boyd agreed as he hit another line

of the good stash. Fathead had separated us out a large pile of the uncut portion, as compensation for cutting up the rest of it in the Waiting Room. Fathead had mixed up a few quick baggies and headed out to drum up business. Boyd continued,

"Fathead is into some dangerous shit. This here is just the tip of the iceberg with that motherfucker."

Big D was nodding along, but you could tell it wasn't sinking in at all. He slid his plate with his newly mixed batch over to Katie who was busily bagging up grams and half grams. She had her glasses out so she could read the scales, and she scowled at Boyd over them. Shut up and let me make us some money, she seemed to say with her glare. We all knew she could really sling some dope when the opportunity arose.

DooWop was busy in the corner, working on his dance moves. He had proclaimed October was to be Michael Jackson month, and was working on mastering as many of the King of Pop's signature moves as he could. He said he preferred to focus on the early stuff, but he had incorporated a little of the pale skinned master's moves as well.

"I could sell that shit for you, be gone in a day if

I take it up to Newberry," he said, pausing in mid gyration.

"No!" everyone but Big D said. DooWop shrugged and went back to the dance.

"Listen, DooWop, you're not getting mixed up in this shit, because then my little brother will be mixed up in it. So no, you got to leave it alone too," Randy explained. Little Bro was at the dad's house for a few days, anyway, but Randy was taking no chances. Randy didn't particularly like cocaine, which was fine with us. Less we had to share.

"I hear you," Big D was saying. "I know. But he's like my only brother I got left now. And he needs my help."

"They ain't no help for that boy, I'm here to tell you. I'm surprised he made it this long, and fucking with this damn cocaine ain't never been good for anybody. They ain't but one way this shit here ever ends up," Betty said sagely from the couch. She had come over to smoke a joint with us and had stayed for the coke party. She wasn't helping with the prep work, but that was all right. At her age, I figured she had already put her time in on this type of shit.

And she was only taking little hits anyway.

Boyd was the one I was worried about. He kept sneaking off to the bathroom to shoot up. The needle was his preferred delivery device for his cocaine, a preference which I agreed with. But since he didn't want everyone to see him shooting up, I couldn't even monitor the levels. I was worried he might make a shot too big one of these times.

Even though I preferred the pin too, I was too lazy to have to hide shooting with this many people around, so I was hitting rails with the rest of the crew.

"Besides, I wasn't even with him when he got this. Fathead flew solo on this caper," Big D assured us. Fathead claimed he had gone to the Biker party down in Four Mile holler at Adam's dad's house. Adam's dad ran the local chapter of the Hell's Angels, and occasionally they passed through and partied at their house down in Four Mile.

And somehow Fathead had come across this kilo of cocaine, apparently just sitting out where any asshole like him could walk off with it. Which he did.

Said he followed the train tracks all the way back to town and caught a ride with Bubbles and Eddie to Middlesboro. He had assured us that they didn't know where he was heading. He had them drop him off at the mall, so nobody knew he had come here. All with a kilo of coke in his backpack.

Fathead did have big ole fat fucking balls.

Still, we felt it prudent to process the coke and get it the hell out of the apartment as soon as possible.

"Fathead takes unnecessary chances, and one day it will catch up with him," I mumbled, turning my attention back to my little pile I was putting up my nose.

There was a knock at the door, low and steady.

"Who the fuck is that?" Boyd demanded as he grabbed his Katana sword and headed to the door. Now, a lot of people might scoff at a shirtless redneck in camouflage shorts high on cocaine brandishing a Katana sword like he meant business.

But those people do so at their peril when it comes to Boyd.

He actually knew how to use the fucking thing. Boyd was an absolute freak with hand weapons. It was the only kind of books he would read, it seemed like, besides voodoo and witch doctor shit. He knew about that shit too, which is probably why he was tapped as curator of Hell's Waiting Room. And while Boyd might have dabbled in the black arts a little bit, he was no expert. But he was an absolute Samurai warrior with his Katana.

I was fishing for a cigarette in case he was going to put on a show with whomever was at the door, when Fathead came bouncing down the hall.

Apparently in to his sample bags he brought, I thought to myself. There is no singularly more judgmental person than a junky in the midst of a coke binge judging another junky's cocaine usage.

Greedy prick, I thought.

"Dog, you will not believe how nuts everybody is going over this shit! I think I cut it just right!" he exclaimed as he crashed down onto the couch, nearly capsizing Katie's work station. She glared at him over the brim of her glasses and pushed the scales over onto the table, spilling cocaine across the faux marble top.

"Hey, hey, hey, dog, watch what the fuck you're doing!" Fathead squealed as he scrambled to clean it up.

"This is important!" he spat out at Katie.

"Importante!" called DooWop from his corner in the midst of spinning around on his head. He had switched to old school break dancing. "Muy Muy importante!" He finished in a split and somehow sprung back to his feet while simultaneously lighting a cigarette.

"That's how my dad says the Columbians call it," he said, exhaling a cloud of smoke.

"Well whatever they call it, dog, be careful. Damn, y'all are some sloppy motherfuckers," Fathead griped as he took over for Katie, who had wandered into the kitchen after hitting the line I offered her. I figured she would want to calm down after Fathead's untimely entrance.

He continued,

"I ran into six or seven heads I know over at the mall and blew all their minds. I'm gonna make a killing. Told them I would find them tomorrow, and to tell their friends. I got the fire!"

"Maybe you should chill the fuck out with that shit," Boyd said absently looking through a copy of "Guns and Ammo."

"Maybe you shouldn't let everybody and they momma know what you're holding."

"Naw, dog, it's cool. I got you," Fathead said with a smile. "Don't worry, Boyd, everything is gonna work out fine. Come on, Big D, let's take a few more samples over to the pool hall and I can sling to the ones you don't hustle."

And grabbing a handful of cocaine filled bundles of joy, Fathead and Big D retired to the pool hall.

"Goddam that little motherfucker makes me a nervous wreck," Betty sighed, lighting another joint.

"Makes me wish I had a Xanax," she said, shaking her head.

Katie wandered over, took the joint Betty offered her, and produced a Xanax out of her pocket with a smile.

"Oh, baby, bless you child. You save an old woman's heart today. I can't take that fuckin Fathead," she said as she reached for her beer to take the pill with. Katie beamed and sat back down at her spot on the couch.

"Oh, Katie, you're such a people pleaser," Randy laughed at her, as she gave him the bird. He smiled and shook his head.

Randy always said they didn't fool around. She had offered, he said, once. And when he told her he wasn't ready to be with anyone yet, she left him alone, he said.

I hoped it was true, what he told us about her being too young and definitely too vulnerable for him to fool with. And she didn't really act like they were fucking. They always acted more like brother and sister, or cousins or something. Maybe just friends of the opposite sex who shared a bedroom; just exactly roommates.

I was always glad for me that she didn't pick my bedroom window to sneak through that night. I was usually too plastered to make such well thought out decisions with my pecker. And I knew I was glad for her that she hadn't tried Boyd that night. Boyd's pecker made zero well thought out decisions whether he was drunk or not. Shacking up in an asexual manner with Randy was probably the best decision Katie could have made.

But I sometimes wondered if it was us or the Room that was making the decisions.

Adam and his father showed up late that night, after we had cleaned up all the cocaine parapher-nalia and evidence. We were being careful with our share Fathead had left us. Didn't want to just binge it all away that first night. And as long as we had other outlets, we were pretty good about ra-tioning.

Luckily, for all of us, Margot had stopped by to smoke some pot, right after Betty had left, and right before Adam and his dad, JT, got there. Adam's dad knew Boyd pretty well, having run around with Boyd's dad, Hippy John back in the day.

"Well come on in here, JT, Adam, welcome, welcome," Boyd greeted them at the door. He was still maintaining a little bit of a cocaine high, as was his way, even though officially we were all done for the evening and had switched to downers. Boyd always did have a dope double standard.

"It's good to see you, but this ain't a social call," JT said as he entered the living room. He quickly surveyed the room and stopped short when he saw us all in there.

"Hello," Margot spoke for the Waiting Room. "How are you this evening? Care for a toke?" she asked offering the joint she had just lit.

"Umm, no, uh, ma'am," JT said. "I didn't know you had company, Boyd. Adam said you would know what we need to know though." He seemed agitated, but was holding it all together pretty well considering he was on the hunt for some thieving bastard who had stolen his kilo of cocaine.

The joint lazily made its way around the room, with DooWop adding one into the mix and Randy producing another one. Katie brought JT and Adam a beer as they told us of their trouble. Adam had settled into the couch next to Margot, and was checking her out, currently off the hunt for the kilo.

JT remained standing and focused on the hunt, politely refusing each joint as they came around. He told Boyd how he thought he might have lost something, something valuable, like he and Hippy John used to handle, and had Boyd heard anything about anything like that?

Boyd said,

"Hippy John hasn't fooled with anything like that in years, definitely nothing like he used to fool with. We just been in here smoking weed all night, trying to figure out somewhere fun to take our lady friends here. You know, JT, that I will let you or Adam know if I hear anything."

"Well, Adam here says you boys hear everything that goes on around here. He says everybody comes by here, and well," JT looked around approvingly, "I can see why. If I was twenty years younger and not tied up this evening I'd stay and show you young'uns how it's really done. Anyways, me and junior here gotta hit the road. There's a couple more places I wanna put the word out. If I catch wind of whoever did this..." and he let out a low whistle while slashing a finger across his throat.

"You get the picture, don't you Boyd?"

"Indeed, I do JT, indeed I do," Boyd answered.

Adam reluctantly got off the couch, hurriedly scribbling his number on a scrap of paper for Margot, in case she happened to hear anything.

She smiled warmly, and tossed the paper at DooWop as Boyd shut the door behind Adam and JT, locking the deadbolt.

We all let out a collective sigh of relief. Except for Katie who smiled and produced a little round mirror, the kind with one side normal and the other side zoomed in so you could really get at those pesky nose hairs. She had lines all ready to go on the cocaine side of the mirror, a rolled-up dollar bill at the order. She proceeded to make her way around the room, serving a line to any and all who wanted one, which of course, was everyone. She came to Boyd last, giving him a little salute as he came up off the line.

"Thank you, Katie, at ease," he said.

"Job well done, everybody. Way to keep your heads. Margot, you have seen too much, and all you need to know is that you have not actually seen anything at all," Boyd concluded.

"Seen what?" she laughed.

"I don't know what you crazy motherfuckers are up to, and I don't really want to know. All I know is I lost my paper with that poor boy's phone number on it even if it did turn out I knew any-thing. Which I don't. Damn, Katie, that shit was good! But I can see y'all got some shit to work out amongst yourselves, so adieu my lovely conspira-tors."

And with that she hugged Katie, kissed DooWop on the forehead, smacked Little Bro lightly on the face when he closed his eyes and puckered his lips, waved at me, gave Randy a fist bump, and kissed Boyd on the cheek on the way out the door.

"Tell Betty I'm sorry I missed her, and I will catch her on the flip side!" she called as she headed out the door, hopped up on surprise cocaine.

Surprise cocaine is the very best kind, after all.

Thirteen

Pavo's Plumbing

When Fathead found out that JT had been to see us, he freaked. Said he wasn't going to sell anything to anybody. Took all the coke and hid out at his house. Didn't even bring us anything over to party with while he was laying low, which was okay. We were having plumbing issues in the Waiting Room anyway.

The plumbing issues started with Pavo. Pavo fancied himself a ladies' man, and I guess the little bastard was. More so than any of the rest of us anyway. He would always show up with a different lady friend, looking for a place to smoke some weed, have a couple of drinks, and work on convincing his lady friend to sleep with him.

We always said the more the merrier, and the Room would always let you know if you weren't welcome.

We were coming off of our coke binge with some weed Betty brought over when Pavo showed up. He had Fleetwood Mac Laura with him.

I had spent an evening trying to get into Fleetwood Mac Laura's pants once, back when I thought she was just Laura. We ended up in her grandmother's house listening to her extensive Fleetwood Mac collection; it was the full set, everything ever put out with Fleetwood Mac's name on it.

It was without a doubt the most singularly horrifying evening of my bachelorhood. Fucking Fleetwood Mac.

Pavo, on the other hand, was not bound by standards such as this. And Fleetwood Mac Laura was hot as fuck. So, nobody gave him too hard a time when he showed up with her.

"Hey everybody," she said, upon entering the Waiting Room. "Wanna put on some Fleetwood Mac and groove for a while?"

Randy grimaced from his spot by the stereo and turned up the Beck. DooWop missed a step when she said it, but he recovered and kept on jamming out to Beck. Old Beck is pretty good, before the cultists got ahold of him.

Katie just shook her head, while Boyd and I gave an emphatic, "Fuck No!" in unison.

Little Bro was just staring at her, as was his way, trying to figure out if he could slip his hand down his pants undetected. Betty smacked him on the back of his head and told him to

"Quit that shit you little fucker!"

Everyone settled in for the blunt that Pavo produced. We had been having a discussion on the difficulties of the release of the cocaine constipation, being as how we only had one toilet in the apartment. I generally didn't get constipated on cocaine, due to the amount of baby laxative you usually had mixed in there. But this coke had been pre-laxative. So I was feeling a might bound up.

Betty had already told us we could not use hers, except for Katie.

"You motherfuckers is nasty, that's why only Katie," she had said.

Pavo was in rare form that particular evening,

telling just enough jokes to keep Fleetwood Mac Laura interested, but not so many as to be annoying. I was impressed with him, as he usually went too far as the annoying guy that thinks he's funny. But that night he was pulling it off.

We needed more beer, so Randy and I went on a bootlegger run. Unfortunately, this meant an hour up to Frakes to Porter's, since Boyd's fake ID had been confiscated over at the Sundowner in Tazewell the previous weekend. Who knew they were actually going to have a bouncer that cared? We had claimed sexism but to no avail.

When we got back from the bootlegger, the Waiting Room was eerily quiet. Boyd and Katie were passing a joint back and forth in silence. The television had snow playing at a low volume. They were the only two in the living room.

"Where is everybody?" I asked.

"Betty went home to pass out, DooWop and Little Bro went to score some marbles for their slingshot at Kmart, and Pavo is trying to fuck Fleetwood Mac Laura in Randy's bedroom," Boyd said while Katie nodded, a look of disgust on her face.

"What?!" Randy exclaimed, marching immediately to his bedroom door and jiggling the lock. He began pounding on the door and calling for them to get the fuck out of his room. Pavo responded by turning up the music on Randy's stereo.

"Go Your Own Way," began to permeate the Waiting Room, met immediately with shouting and cursing from those of us in the peanut gallery. I laughed a little under my breath, though. Fucking Fleetwood Mac.

"Open this goddam door you son of a bitch!" Randy was yelling and beating on the door.

"You can't do it no good with that little pecker you're packing anyway you little dick motherfucker!" The music got louder, and we began to fear Randy might break the door down.

Boyd asked Katie if her window was unlocked, and headed for the balcony when she nodded in the affirmative. But before he made it outside, the door swung open to reveal Pavo, in a tiny cutoff t-shirt and boxer shorts. He was missing one sock.

"What's going on, man?" he asked nonchalantly, ducking under Randy's swipe at his head as he dodged his way into the bathroom. Fleetwood Mac Laura emerged fully clothed in her typical hippy dress, looking none the worse for wear, with a look of extraordinary boredom on her face. She waltzed into the living room and sat down next to Katie, lighting a smoke.

"That was disappointing," she said simply, to Katie, who burst into laughter.

"It's not fucking funny!" Randy was shouting from inside his room. He managed to get the go-dawful Fleetwood Mac off the stereo, much to the delight of everyone else.

"Pavo, you better not be flushing any condoms in there!" Boyd called as the toilet flushed. Pavo didn't respond, but instead flushed again as soon as the tank refilled.

"Pavo, I fucking mean it!" Boyd yelled again. He rose to confront Pavo at the bathroom door, as he emerged sheepishly.

"No, of course not, Boyd, I know better than that," he said as he started gathering up his clothes that Randy was flinging from his room. The Fleetwood Mac had been replaced with obscene cursing that bordered on emotional abuse.

Looking embarrassed a little bit, Pavo slipped his clothes back on, except for his shoes, which Randy had decided to throw out the window down to the parking lot.

"You wanna get out of here?" he said to Laura as he buckled his pants.

"You go ahead, hon, I'm gonna hang here a while," she said indifferently. She was busy braiding Katie's hair, who looked to be thoroughly enjoying having someone play with her long auburn hair. Pavo made a face, and beat a hasty retreat, which was probably wise because Randy was starting to go through the sheets and was beginning to threaten castration.

Boyd was making a weird face, and with a little moan, headed to the bathroom. The cocaine constipation had worn off, it looked like.

I set about rolling a couple of joints and sipping my beer while I asked Katie and Laura what they wanted to hear on the radio, besides Fleetwood Mac of course. After a while, Boyd flushed the toilet. And proceeded to yell and curse and flip out. I picked myself up off the couch and knocked on the door to see if he was alright. He flung the door open, face red and streaming with sweat.

"The fucking toilet is clogged, man. And I am not making any headway with this piece of shit plunger!" he exclaimed. The plunger looked as if it had been through a war zone, battle scars all up and down the handle. The toilet was full to the brim with brown nastiness. At least he had turned off the fill valve.

"I'll go see if Betty has one we can borrow," I said, smiling discreetly. I was glad it was Boyd's mess to clean up. I returned with Betty's premiere plunger, (it had a little caddy for it and everything), and with a big grin, I said,

"Your weapon, good sir."

Boyd glared at me and went back into battle, muttering under his breath about how everybody is a fucking comedian when the shitter's full. I laughed as I lit my joint and settled in to watching Katie and Laura, who were huddled on the little couch, whispering and giggling. It made me smile, because I felt like Katie could use more girls in her life. She's always just hanging with us, just one of the guys, I thought. It was sweet seeing her be all girly.

I stopped smiling when Boyd emerged from the shitter.

"It's fucked," he said simply as he grabbed a beer and fell down onto the couch. "I can't do anything with it."

I assured him it was due to his inferior training

in the custodial arts, and that I could take care of it once I got my mind right.

Five beers and two joints later, I was ready to tackle the job.

Boyd was right. Shitter was fucked. After about an hour, we decided we would have to ask Saul to snake it or something.

Unfortunately, since it was Friday afternoon, Saul was nowhere to be found. We knew we wouldn't see that motherfucker until Monday, so we started working on a plan for the weekend.

I could feel my own cocaine constipation waning, and I knew I wasn't waiting until Monday. Never mind Randy, who had no bowel discipline at all anyway.

We were talking about how fucked up it was that we couldn't get any maintenance work done on weekends. Although, to be fair, we knew damn well we didn't live in the kind of place that would provide weekend maintenance, and it was well reflected in the monthly rent. Just then, DooWop and Little Bro showed up, looking like they had been in some sort of a scrape.

"What the fuck happened to you two?" Randy demanded of his brother.

"It was crazy," Little Bro began. "We was just minding our own business, when these two- "

"Three," DooWop cut in, "three big ass motherfuckers came out of nowhere. They said we had busted their grandma's window-"

"Allegedly!" Little Bro interrupted. "And they said they were gonna beat our brains out, and then they jumped us-"

"Sucker punched us," DooWop interjected, "and we were outnumbered and they were bigger than us-"

"But then, this wild looking Mexican came out of nowhere and smacked one of them with a hammer, and kicked the other one, and the third one ran off!" Little Bro finished the tale.

"Mexican?" Boyd asked. "Did you know him?"

"It was none other than Wile E. Coyote!" DooWop answered. There was a general sigh of disbelief that emanated out of each of us.

"The Phantom Stroker?" Boyd asked, obviously in shock.

"The Mystery Ejaculator?" Laura said, smiling brightly and nudging Katie, who giggled.

Before they could answer in the affirmative, Randy intervened.

"Well, you two little motherfuckers are lucky that Mexican came around. Stop breaking windows, goddamit!" Randy instructed, to which they both protested that they hadn't even been breaking windows today.

Katie brought some ice for DooWop's eye, and Fleetwood Mac Laura prepared an herb and spice poultice from some shit she had in her hippy bag for Little Bro to put on his lip and everyone calmed down with an interjection of marijuana.

I forgot the toilet was even broken, until the middle of the night, when it came at me all at once. Stimulants make some of us constipated, sometimes for days and days after we come off a bender. They do a number on your libido as well, but that was a different problem.

I awoke in the middle of the night with unbearable pain in my gut. For a moment I wondered what a burst appendix felt like, but then the bowels began to move and I knew what was happening. Had to get to the toilet, quick.

Someone had beaten me to it.

I flung open the toilet seat and was greeted with an unconscionable stench. The excrement that was working its way through my lower intestine at a rapid rate threatened to reverse course and come out through the other end. I gagged and held my hand over my mouth, slamming the toilet lid back down.

I saw the tub, and I had a thought for a moment, but dismissed it as quickly as it had come. I frantically glanced around the tiny bathroom. There was only the sink left as a porcelain receptacle. It was one of those wall hanging sinks, where the pipe comes out the bottom and curves into the wall. For a moment I envisioned disconnecting the sink pipe and shitting directly down the tube to the sewer. But I knew from the rumbling in my belly I didn't have that kind of time.

We were nearing the event horizon and I was contemplating just shitting over the edge of the balcony, cars below be damned, when my frantically searching eye settled on the trash can next to the toilet. It was a Spiderman trash can, DooWop's contribution to the bathroom décor. We previously had one that was a sort of doody brown color, and as I dropped my drawers and hovered over the Spiderman trash can I thought about the sick irony of having replaced a doody brown trash can with a Spiderman one, only to have to now fill the Spiderman one with doody brown doody.

It was a glorious experience, relief at long last. I was gripping the edge of the sink, for balance, when Boyd stuck his head in.

"Everything ok—Jesus!" he exclaimed and slammed the door. Serves him right, the nosy motherfucker.

"Good God, man, is that the trash can? DooWop is gonna be pissed!" he yelled through the door, but I could tell he was laughing.

"What are you going to do with it after?"

"I don't know. Fuck off!" I yelled through the door.

"I was only in the planning stages when it happened!"

I heard Boyd lean against the door and light a smoke. Why was this asshole up in the middle of the night anyway?

Oh yeah. Cocaine.

"Well, it seems to me we could just take it down there and dump it in the dumpster. Then hose out the trash can for another round?" Boyd queried.

I had completed the task and was washing my hands when he came back in. Luckily, Katie, or someone with sense, had placed a plastic grocery bag in the trash can and tied it tight on the side to hold it in place. It had worked fairly well, and I had then loosened the bag from the trash can and neatly tied it closed on top. Little bag of shit inside a Spiderman trash can, pretty as you please.

"Wow, that is a very tidy package you've prepared there," Boyd commented.

"Purely by accident, but it does give me an idea," I said, grabbing the can and heading toward the door.

"What have you got planned, you crazy bastard?" Boyd asked as he followed me to the door.

As we passed Randy's room, we heard him call out,

"What the fuck is going on out there?"

"Bag of shit. Spiderman," Boyd responded, which must have made sense to Randy because he apparently went back to sleep.

When we got out onto the balcony, my plan was foiled. I had been planning to bring the can down to the dumpster and throw the bag of shit away. But it was raining cats and dogs.

"Well, shit." I said defeatedly.

"I got you," Boyd said simply. He reached into

the can, grabbed the handles of the tied off Save-a-Lot bag, took a crow hop toward the end of the balcony swinging the bag in a little circle, like a spinning sling of shit, and as he landed his hop, with the arc of the shit sack swinging up, he released it.

The bag of shit flew like an overweight lumbering swan trying to reach and maintain altitude with a body nearly too big for aerodynamics, a massive pile of shit wrapped in plastic with the handles of the Save-a-Lot bag trailing frantically behind it. It flew almost, nearly far enough to hit the dumpster, although the top was down, so it wouldn't have made it in anyway. It ended up short, landing with a wet splat on the pavement.

"Short armed it," Boyd muttered disgustedly.

"Well, better luck next time," I said with a smile.

And thus, a new sport we dubbed Flying Shit Stain, was born. Surprisingly, Randy turned out to be the best shit slinger of us all, a real natural talent with a twirling bag of doody.

We sent Little Bro down to open the top for us the next morning. I went with him to scoop my bag of shit into the dumpster using Saul's shovel I found leaning in the alley. We spent the rest of the weekend trying to shit just so we could throw the bags from the balcony.

Randy suggested we call everyone up to come over and shit in Spiderman for us, but we voted him down. People thought we were weird enough already.

Saul arrived first thing Monday morning. He had apparently heard about the shit sack throwing competition, and was not amused. He was cussing us in Spanish while he snaked the toilet, eventually producing, predictably, a used condom.

"Fucking Pavo" we all said in unison, although we were all a little disappointed that we had to go back to shitting in the toilet.

Fourteen

The Nurse Comes Calling

All weekend we had been discussing, in between rounds of shit throwing, the anomaly that was the Waiting Room. Everyone was just sort of stuck there, it seemed. Randy was convinced that the Room was allowing him to leave, by way of the military in a few short weeks, because he finally had his mind right. He felt Boyd and I must still have some unresolved issues buried deep in our psyches that had prevented the Room from allowing our departure with him.

"Yeah, maybe, and maybe it's because the slowest metabolism known to man over here can't pass a drug test," Boyd retorted, gesturing toward me.

"And anyway, I think when something new comes along that we are supposed to do, we'll do it. We're just marking time right now, waiting. Hence the name of the Room," Boyd concluded.

I agreed, to a certain extent. I didn't feel trapped by the Room, but I had witnessed many a visitor appear to get trapped, at least for a day or two. There was always somebody with car trouble that ended up staying the night, or a runaway hiding out for a day or two, or a junky with nowhere to go for a few days. Even Margot had mentioned the phenomenon a time or two, that it seemed that no matter how long she planned to stay when she came over, it always seemed to be determined by forces outside her control. She had finally just given up on making her curfew.

And numerous people had sat down on the couch and seemed unable to leave and also unable to refrain from disclosing all sorts of their most private and personal shit.

"Yeah, and maybe it's the drugs," I said instead. Katie nodded her agreement, but I wasn't so sure she was really free to leave either. Where would she go, after all? Back to her family home where the brother pimps her out and the mom is a complicit terror in her own right?

And Little Bro? Randy had moved out of his widower Dad's house, for good reason. Their dad was a drunk prick, and everyone could see they were better off away from him. He had already driven the mother to suicide. But where did that leave Little Bro?

We had come up with the Hell's Waiting Room idea on the first night on some heavy-duty acid we got off Jerome for a house warming present. Jerome always had good acid. He mixed it up himself, he claimed, and we didn't really have any reason to doubt him other than he seemed like a dumbass. So, we had our doubts a little bit, but we still always took the acid when he showed up.

We had been in there tripping in the dark, when it started to come to Boyd, about hell having a waiting room and what it would look like. We all pitched in ideas about how it would be shitty, but not too shitty, because they had to save most of the true torture for the actual hell.

Randy had said we should name the Nurse, and kept calling her Nurse Ratchet from Kill Bill. Boyd tried to explain that Nurse Ratchet was from One Flew Over the Cuckoo's Nest, which led to a discussion on Kesey and the Pranksters which ended with us huffing neon paint and listening to the Grateful Dead all night.

And in the morning, we awoke to Randy talking to the Sky Lizard. He who had been up all night with the paint can and a slew of bread bags. He kept ripping them open and letting the paint drip all over the carpet in his meditation station at the wall of the Lizard. That was how the couch ended up permanently parked there even though it was slightly longer than the wall and stuck out into the hallway ever so slightly. We didn't want Saul to see all the paint on the carpet. Of course, that was to be the least of his worries on turning that apartment when we were done with it.

But the idea of the Waiting Room stuck after that night. We would laugh to ourselves about the shoddy conditions and lack of quality entertainment, and it made sense that people only wanted to come there because it was slightly less awful than the hell that was their everyday lives. Until something or someone, usually a form of the

Nurse, calls their name and leads them on to the next level of hell.

Chicago Shelly came to get DooWop.

"Hey y'all," she said when Randy let her in. "DooWop home?"

"Hey Momma," he said from the corner, pausing in mid stutter step spin.

"Can you come back to our house for a while? Your daddy is getting out today, and it would be really great if we were all there to meet him when he gets home. You know," she said simply.

DooWop mumbled his consent and told us he would be back in a couple of days and walked through that door for the last time. None of us realized it, which was typical of how it happens. You don't always know for sure when somebody has been called for, and you don't think to tell them goodbye.

Fifteen

Jerome

It didn't start that way, but it turned into a bad trip.

Jerome had shown up with some acid. Jerome was Mel's friend. Mel never came to the Waiting Room. She did once, and said it freaked her out. It was all too close, she told us.

We figured she meant the other side was too close, because we felt it too. In any case, she never came back. Although, since she was a drug dealer, and the bulk of her business was done out of her home, it is possible that she didn't get out much anyway.

Jerome was Mel's friend that followed the Dead around. At least he used to, back in the day, he said. These days he mostly just went from one outdoor festival to another, trading in acid and other controlled substances to cover his various tickets and accommodations.

He didn't require much in the way of accommodations, it seemed, preferring to sleep outdoors if it was warm enough. So, most of his profits went to supporting his prodigious drug habit. Jerome was the one guy that even we struggled to keep up with.

He had made the Waiting Room a regular stop on his cross-country treks following the folk festivals du jour. He would dutifully telephone Mel every time to tell her he was in town, and ask her to come over to the Waiting Room to see him. She would always come up with some lame excuse, and after a couple of days with us he would make me drive him all the way out to Mel's place in Pineville. It wasn't really that far, but when you were fucked up from a bender with Jerome it felt like forever.

He had shown up this time with acid, which was typical.

"Mel. Baby. You gotta check this shit out. You won't believe it. Maaaaaan."

Jerome always talked really, really slow. Like he was working out in great detail the next word that would proceed from his lips.

Only the words were never that big, in my opinion, and shouldn't have taken that long to form. He was doing a lot more drugs than the rest of us, though, I suppose.

"Stop. Maaaaan. I know what you're thinking."

He probably did.

"you're thinking. Can this.....shit. Be... as. Gooooooood. As he says?"

Only one way to find out, I thought.

"Only. One. Way. To. Find. Out." He agreed.

And we were off.

When you're on acid it all makes sense. All of it. Everything is connected to everything and you can see it all. And you're also flying. If that's what you want. It can be calm and surreal, if you know how to handle it. Or it can be ecstatically insane at one thousand horrors a minute.

A lot of it depends on who you're on the trip

with. Boyd and I could always find each other and share the same trip. Randy would come in and out of the trip with us, but he was never really in our it, not of his own volition of course. When Randy figured everything out about it, the it was always about him being alone. He never fully trusted us, and on acid, this is part of the it he would figure out.

We could usually bring other heads in the room into our orbit, on the trip. We could usually help everyone have a good time. A lot of that was mitigating Randy's private interactions with the guests. He scared people a lot when he was tripping. I didn't worry about him too much, in regards to me or Boyd, because while he might not fully trust us, the it he would figure out also let him know we loved him and he loved us. Randy was on a weird trip. Always.

With Jerome in the huddle, though, the trip was always more fun. He would play the music, tune after tune that you didn't even know you had over there in the pile, masterfully put together in the most random of playlists that somehow fit together perfectly to compliment the conversation and overall mood in the room.

And when he was running a trip, Jerome became alive. His speech patterns altered, his words gained in speed and rhythm, his cadence drawing you into the discussion at hand on the problems of society, or the future of artistic expression, or the size of a penny, or the smell of a rainbow.

We were dealing Rummy that night, although Randy kept calling it gin and making up new rules as we went along, and Boyd was playing a side hand of blackjack with Katie, and Jerome was teaching us the intricacies of Texas Hold 'em, which is different if it has a little e in the 'em as opposed to the traditional Big E in the 'Em. At least according to Jerome, which made perfect sense; until there was a knock at the door.

It started loud, I thought, but no one else seemed to hear it. Only the Sky Lizard, who nodded toward the door and winked, understood in his lizard way that there was a disturbance in our trip.

I told everyone that I would get the door, but my voice and I were in a fight, which happened sometimes. It couldn't keep up with the rest of me, and couldn't move through my vocal cords at the correct speed to correspond with my thoughts.

My voice did this sometimes, as a prank. It wasn't very funny, I would tell it, which it would announce much later, when the moment had passed.

Who is it? I tried to ask through the door, but my voice did not comply. I thought of the steps Ivan would have to go through to install a security system for us that actually worked, not like the ones he gave to Shell stations, and all of his annoying complaints and the incessant bitching that would go on were we to contract him to perform such a task, and realized that it would not help in the current situation with the overanxious door-knocker who was growing more insistent by the millisecond, and so I said, Fuck It, which my voice failed to enunciate.

I opened the door.

The State Trooper's Smokey the Bear hat was two sizes too small. And he didn't look jovial or mischievous. Not like Smokey the Bear at all, who I had transposed into Yogi Bear in my mind through all the connections that only I could see.

I could explain it to him, but he wouldn't get it. Plus, he was a cop.

It's the Police, I called to the Waiting Room,

by way of warning, but my voice was still playing around and wouldn't help me.

"Are you Randy Jenkins?" he asked in a voice that seemed too high for such a large head. The muscles bulged in his neck, squeezing his vocal cords until they were mere squeaks of themselves. I wondered if his voice got mad at squeaking through such tight quarters and went on strike like mine did.

His voice would be justified in such an uprising. My voice was just a whiny bitch.

"Boo fucking Hoo," I said to my voice, who decided to make an appearance. What a dick.

"What?!" the cop demanded, his high voice getting shriller as his vocal cords were further tightened by the blood vessels expanding to let more blood flow to his face, which had become a crimson nightmare.

"Wait right out here, Boo Boo, I'll just fetch Mr. Jenkins and a pic-a-nic basket," I said in my best Yogi the Bear imitation, my voice cooperating just this once.

I stood in the doorway and called over my shoulder,

"Randy, this policeman would like a word!"

"What?!" Boyd yelled back, Three Dog Night playing in the background.

Momma did tell me not to come, I thought. Fucking Jerome, on point as always, I thought with a smile.

The record screeched to a stop, and Jerome put on Beastie Boys, Sabotage. At least he didn't put on Fuck the Police I thought, as my voice tried its best to sing that song instead, but I was currently in charge of the vocal cords.

"Who's in charge here?" I asked my voice, all proud of myself.

Smokey the Yogi Bear raised his eyebrows, which made his tiny hat shrink by two more sizes.

"Holy Shit, man, it is the fucking cops! Far. Fucking. Out Maaaaaaan!" Jerome had poked his head around the corner so he could see down the hall to the doorway.

Randy's artwork on the wall halfway down the hallway caught his eye, which I knew was going to be a mistake. That fucking head on a snake body wrapping itself around a soul was its own fucked up trip, in the best of times.

And this was not the best of times. Jerome trailed off, caught in the web of artistic entrapment that only Randy could dream up. Which, perhaps, was the point of the awful thing, as it gave Randy time to pop around the corner.

He looked cool, calm, and collected as he came to the door, which I suppose made up for me looking concerned, crazed, and cornered.

"Good evening, sir, how can I help you," he said in perfect English.

English was a good choice, I thought. I snapped my head around to see how Yogi would take it.

"Sir," Yogi said, "you are listed as the contact for a minor, Joshua Jenkins. He says you are his brother. We tried to contact his father but were unsuccessful. There's been an incident. I think you better come with me."

Randy agreed that he should, which sounded like a horrible idea to me, but my voice was fucking around again, so I couldn't warn him, and Randy left with Smoky Yogi the Bear Cop to find out the nature of the aforementioned incident.

Turns out Little Bro had seen some shit. And done some shit.

Chicago Shelly had been right. Everett had gotten his release. They had a big welcome home party for him, which consisted mostly of Shelly and

Everett smoking a lot of crack and screaming at the kids. And when they ran out of crack to smoke, Everett had decided to bring DooWop to go get another rock.

Being newly released from jail, Everett was strapped for cash. So, he went to old reliable, Shoot 'Em Up Shell over on Catalpa, the one with Ivan's special installation cameras. Except since he was just home from jail on suspicion of robbing said Shell station, Everett gave DooWop the pistol and sent him in to score the cash.

Hakim the Grocer knew his video surveillance didn't work, due to shoddy American workmanship he assumed. He had taken other measures. DooWop took two in the chest from the little snubby .38 that Hakim had gotten from his cousin, who knew where to get such things.

Hakim paid $150 for it. Hakim had about $178 in the register, give or take. So, all told, DooWop's life cost about $328, give or take.

Little Bro had been watching from outside in the bushes. He had followed for moral support, and to try to help DooWop fight off Everett if it came to that. DooWop and Little Bro were tight that way. Do anything for a friend.

When Little Bro saw DooWop fall, he reached in his backpack and pulled out Randy's Glock .40 that he had lifted when he passed through that afternoon. We hadn't really noticed him, although Jerome played Johnny Cash's Leave your Guns at Home.

Jerome was always on.

Little Bro shot Hakim three times, once in the abdomen, once in the shoulder, and once in the head as he stood over him. Ivan cleaned up the video for Boyd and me to watch one night and it was chilling.

Little Bro looked outside, and I believe if Everett would have stuck around, he would have gotten three shots too. Then Little Bro sat down next to DooWop, held his head in his lap and talked to him, silently for us as Ivan's shoddy video had no sound, until the police arrived.

They put him in the back of the squad car and started trying to figure out who to call about this kid who just participated in a double homicide. Middlesboro PD is not equipped for such a case; thus, Smokey had been called in from the State Police Barracks to take over.

By the time Randy got home from the station,

and told us the news, Jerome had split. Betty brought over some weed and hugged on Randy so he could cry into her shoulder. Boyd, Katie, and I sat in stunned silence, with Katie finally joining in the hug fest with Randy and Betty.

Jerome had left Don Mclean in the machine for us, the "Day the Music Died."

All I heard was the little chef. Bam. Bam. Bam. Over and over, like the gunshot anthem of the Shoot 'Em Up Shell.

Sixteen

Uncle Calvin

We had six days to agonize before the funeral. Betty explained to us.

"You white folks bury your dead too soon. You got to let the body lie out, so people can pay they respects. Y'all always wanting to hurry up and get granny in the ground so we can start selling her house and spending her money. *We* know they ain't gonna be no damn money and the motherfuckin bank gonna sell that house and keep what money there is. So we ain't in a hurry to bury nobody. Cause fuck a bank."

I didn't think she was wrong, necessarily, and I damn sure wasn't going to argue with her either way. The main thing is DooWop's funeral wasn't going to be for a few days. Chicago Shelly had his body up at her house, laid out, as Betty had said it would be. We went on day two of the festivities.

It was hard, seeing him there. Dead. He was only twelve or so, best as we could figure. I didn't dare ask his mother at this late stage in our relationship. She already thought Randy was simple because she didn't get his sense of humor. And he could be simple sometimes. But I didn't want her to think she had failed in her parental responsibility by letting her boy spend so much time around a bunch of mentally challenged drug addicts.

It was bad enough we were drug addicts.

I found myself hating Everett, the father of the year. But I also found myself wondering what kind of a father any of the rest of us could possibly be. Randy would probably be a good dad, but Boyd and me? Doubtful.

I'd at least had a fatherly example growing up. My dad didn't drink or smoke or even really cuss. He was a Baptist preacher and really did try to walk the walk. But Boyd's daddy was a lot like us, a junky, a petty criminal, a drunk, and a fuckup. I sort of felt like we might be more like him than my dad, when it came to paternal responsibility.

And Boyd's dad was fucked up. He most certainly was. Very violent and dangerous when he was in "one of his ways", as Boyd's mom put it. Hippy John was called Hippy John, not for his free lovin' peacenik ways, which didn't really exist, but because of his freewheeling drug use.

He beat on the whole family quite a bit, and started in with weapons early on, just in case Boyd ever started getting too big for his britches. The whole impetus for us moving into the Waiting Room in the first place was because Boyd's mom realized Boyd and Hippy John were liable to kill each other at any minute. Hippy john had started Boyd off too early in weapons training, and now Boyd was faster with a knife and a better shot, and Hippy John was struggling with accepting this development more and more.

It did make me feel a little guilty at times, realizing how easy it was at my house growing up, compared to seemingly everyone else. Especially that day, seeing DooWop lying there, dead, in his momma's living room. It made me worry about what kind of father I would be, if it ever came to that.

I had to get outside to get some air, and choke down a cigarette. And fight back tears.

I found Randy learning how to shoot dice with DooWop's uncle Calvin and a few other cousins and family members. It seemed to only be family at the house.

DooWop always said Uncle Calvin was his very favorite uncle.

"You another one of DooWop's roommates, like this cracker here?" Uncle Calvin asked. He smiled when he said it, to let me know that he was breaking my balls a little bit for being one of the only white guys, but also to let me know I was still a crackerass cracker. He was quickly becoming my favorite uncle too.

"I guess so," I said, "to both."

Calvin raised his eyebrows, and loosened his silk tie a little at the neck. It was hot out, and it was a nice tie. It's swirl of turquoise and purple matched the pocket square, and the pinstripe in his charcoal black three-piece suit. A silver pocket watch chain was sweeping in grand fashion from the pocket of the vest.

"Roommate and cracker," I said with a grin. One of the other cousins looked up sharply, glaring at me from under his ballcap. Another one stood up and took a step forward, presumably to protect Uncle Calvin from this smart mouth white boy.

Uncle Calvin didn't look like he was the type of guy to need anybody protecting him from the likes of a whitebread cracker like me, but it didn't matter. He broke out into a grin and stuck out his hand, grabbing mine in a tight squeeze.

"DooWop told me you boys always looked out for him. I knew it was better for him to be over there than with this no-good sumbitch my sister shacked up with," he said, anger and frustration washing over his face. Uncle on his momma's side. No wonder DooWop liked him. This was obviously the superior side of the gene pool.

"And this one's brother," he released my hand and gestured over to Randy,

"This young man's brother avenged DooWop's death, and though violence only begets more violence and through this violence we will never have peace, this young man's brother made a gesture so important, so vital, so honest, that it showed his true colors, that of being a true brother to his fellow man."

There were murmurings of "preach" and "tell it brother Cal" and "fuck them Pakistanis" that made their way through the crowd that was gathering. I wasn't entirely sure that Little Bro killing Hakim was necessarily any more meaningful than any friend avenging his best friend's death, and I wasn't even really sure it was a justified vengeance in that they were robbing the Shoot 'Em Up Shell at the time. I also wasn't even sure if Hakim was from Pakistan. But I wasn't about to argue in the midst of what was beginning to turn into a pretty lively time at DooWop's wake.

As Calvin extoled the virtues of young DooWop and his cracker friends, the booze had arrived and the bar was open. There was all sorts of different liquors and beers and hooch and somebody had started rolling blunts and I wasn't about to get us thrown out of this party on account of my own struggle with how I felt about all the killing.

I had done some unsightly things to some people over the years, in the field of battle, but I hadn't killed anyone. To be honest, I was struggling with it a little bit. But this was a serious party, and who was I to sully DooWop's celebration?

I got a beer and intercepted Katie as she was grabbing a blunt and we walked around to the side of the building to get some air. I told her about how SSgt. Jones had come by the apartment, since he was helping Randy with getting a lawyer and mounting a defense for Little Bro.

"Now look, goddamit, this is serious shit your brother is in, here, Randy," he had said.

"But I think we've got a shot, if we can show how you are going in the Marines, and your friends here-", he nodded at Boyd and me, before continuing,

"-are also going in, and how with your mother dead and your dad a drunk, you three amigos are all your little brother has in the world. And he's going to enroll in military school, there's a spot out in a great facility in Utah, guy owes me a favor." He continued,

"I can get him in, get him some work study to cover his room and board. We can convince a judge you are a military family, the whole lot of yous are serving your country, your brother will be ready to matriculate to the Corps on his 18th birthday.

Don't send this young man to prison for the rest of his life. We're gonna shape him up and send him out to fight ragheads. Don't you understand what's at stake, Your Honor?"

I told Katie,

"SSgt. Jones had been standing at this point, pacing the living room like he was giving the closing remarks at Little Bro's trial. He is right, it could work. Little Bro is a white kid, after all, with a tragic home life that is about to be cleaned up by the United States Marine Corps. If the judge is in to veterans and shit, it has a shot."

Katie looked at me while she hit the blunt, an exasperated look on her face.

"Why should it matter what color he is?" she asked, exhaling and reaching for her beer. When she did talk, Katie always made sense.

I didn't say anything. I don't know why it matters, but it sure fucking does. If DooWop and Little Bro were reversed, DooWop would be doing life as an adult. Kill a hardworking entrepreneurial business owner who is legally defending his place of business by exercising his Second Amendment Rights? Shit. That little black kid is fucked in that scenario.

But Little Bro has a shot, cause he's white, and his whole extended family will join the military to be bullet bait if it will get him off. We are at war, after all, your Honor. I mean, aren't we always at war, your Honor? It is a fucked up system, with a certain amount of racism baked right into it.

Of course, this was all predicated on Boyd having to repass his drug test and getting readmitted, and me passing a drug test for the first time ever. Although SSgt. Jones hinted at trying to find a workaround if we had to. Whatever that meant.

All to help Little Bro, I guess.

The irony of having this half monologue conversation with Katie while I was smoking weed was not lost on me. Maybe I'd quit tomorrow, I thought. Or maybe Jones will have to figure out his fucking workaround.

As we were leaving the wake, I heard a weird, white voice call out, "Wait, wait, can I ask you a question?"

"You just di- ", I stopped short as I turned around mid-comeback and was face to face with a Catholic priest. Collar and everything, just like you see on TV, if you grow up Baptist. Mostly on shit like Exorcist when they have to call in the big guns.

Luckily Boyd took the lead, as I had never seen a priest in real life, and had too many rude questions about child molestation.

"Sure, Father, what can we do for you?" Boyd said, all smiles.

He did always enjoy meeting new clergymen. He would usually toy with them a while, then break out his antireligious proclivities. It always got the holler preachers fucked around. We figured they weren't used to somebody who had read a book in addition to the Bible, and he would always give the old college try to fuck with their faith.

And this was a real live Catholic, which we didn't get a lot of in that neck of the woods. Apparently, DooWop was Catholic, or the young priest here had heard the party going and stopped in for a drink.

"I was wondering if you could give me a ride this fine evening? I didn't drive tonight because I knew I would be drinking," he said with a smile.

Randy belched, quite loudly, which caused Katie to start laughing, and I slurred,

"Oh sure, Padre, just gotta remember where I

parked the car," at which point I staggered and veered away from the group, which was only slightly a joke.

I was actually good and drunk. Not so drunk I wasn't going to drive, but this preacher should know his high and mighty drinking and driving policy didn't operate freely here.

"Father...?" Boyd began, pausing for the priest to fill in his own name, which seemed to confuse him slightly.

"Timothy?" the priest answered, looking a little nervously at the rest of us. Boyd seemed to put him at ease, though, as he said,

"Father Timothy, I would be honored to volunteer Jack's humble chariot, to be at your disposal for the purposes of a ride home."

Father Timothy beamed, relieved that he had gotten his name right. And that he had found a ride. We introduced ourselves and continued on back to the apartment to get the car. I actually hadn't driven to the wake because Betty told me the police sometimes watch Black peoples' wakes for DUI. I didn't really want to drink and drive either, but Boyd had volunteered me for the Lord's work, apparently.

I had heard that's how it happens, sometimes, with the Lord's work.

Seventeen

They don't even use hunchbacks no more, not even at funerals

Father Timothy turned out to be pretty friendly, although he didn't want to go into the Waiting Room. We had walked back from DooWop's wake, and we invited Fr. Timothy up for a drink. I had to go up to get the keys anyway.

But when we got to the door, Father Timothy stopped short. He even took a step back. Randy and Katie had already gone inside, Boyd was holding the door, and I was bringing up the rear.

"Umm, okay, umm," the priest said. Boyd just looked at him innocently.

"Everything ok, Father?" he asked sweetly.

"Ummm," he said again.

I decided to come to his rescue,

"It is late, after all, so maybe I'll just grab the keys and we can head out, what do you say, Padre? Another time for the drink, then?"

"Yes, yes," he said, relief beginning to make its way through the color of his face.

"I'll just be a minute," I said, as I brushed past him and entered the apartment.

"What's his problem, not coming in after all?" Randy asked as I grabbed a couple of beers for the road. In case the theory of alcoholic priests holds true, I told myself, secretly hoping that he wouldn't want one and they could both be for me.

I shrugged at Randy, and headed back outside, keys jangling in my pocket. I heard Randy explaining to Katie that Catholic priests were pederasts and you shouldn't really let them in the house any more than you should let Boy Scouts in the house. The great thing about Mute Katie was that she wouldn't argue with any of the crazy shit you might say. Definitely a good listener.

When I got back outside, Boyd was knee deep in a discussion about Apostolic succession,

"and if the sacramental seal that is placed on your heart at ordination is permanent, and if it had been a valid transfer through the laying on of hands from Saint Peter all the way down to the Bishops and priests, and if Martin Luther and the other Reformers had been validly ordained, then wouldn't the succession also continue down through them to at least some of these Protestant preachers out here, being as how hands could be traced all the way back to the Reformation in some cases, and thus back to Saint Peter himself?

"Because aren't the power and presence and seal of the Holy Spirit bigger and more powerful and more permanent than the whimsy of the bishops of Rome?" he finished with a flourish. I honestly don't know where Boyd picked this type of shit up.

Fr. Timothy was clearly enjoying this robust discussion, which pleased Boyd. It was always better if his adversaries thought they had a chance. If they were the type to enjoy a lively debate, of course. Boyd was a debating motherfucker.

"I need to look into that to get you the most accurate answer, but I would love to continue this discussion, Boyd, maybe stop by after Mass any day this week?"

"I will think about it, Father Tim," Boyd said with a smile. It was an actual, genuine smile, and I could tell he liked the young priest. Which was good, in my opinion. Boyd could use a religious friend.

I myself had no real need for religion, but I was interested to hear what Fr. Timothy thought about the Waiting Room. I had an inkling of why he hadn't entered, and I wanted to try to draw it out of him. I couldn't believe Boyd hadn't already gone there.

"So tell me, Padre, what happened up there at the doorway?" I began as soon as he shut his door. I already had us in gear and was pulling out of the parking lot while he fought with the safety belt.

"Ummm, what do you mean?" he tried to play dumb.

"Don't give me that shit, buddy," I scolded,

"I saw you not want to go in. Why is that? Honestly?"

Father Timothy took a deep breath, settled into his seat, and began to tell me his newly forming theory on the Waiting Room, mostly consisting of explaining the Church's current endeavors of downplaying demonic phenomenon, but that there were a small group of 'deliverance priests' he called it, who still worked on delivering people from demonic forces through intercessory prayer and minor exorcisms.

He told me how he had felt something at the apartment, and he didn't think he was prepared at that time to encounter it. Something about needing to receive Communion before engaging in the spiritual warfare battle against evil.

So, like the rest of us, he had felt...something, I thought to myself.

"Deliverance priests?" I asked when he had finished.

"Have you seen the movie? I feel like y'all got enough negative press on you and sexual deviance without naming yourselves after a film synonymous with redneck rape."

He laughed, and said he agreed with the sentiment, but that in Latin it sounded much better.

"Do you ever feel anything in the apartment?" he asked, his face all seriousness.

"Well, Padre, to be honest with you, I'm pretty loaded most of the time. I feel all kinds of shit. But

I do know what you mean, a sort of presence or something," I began.

And then, I guess because I wasn't Catholic and wasn't freaked out about confession, I told him all about Hell's Waiting Room. I figured he wasn't allowed to tell anyone anyway, right? I told him about how it sometimes seemed to have a mind of its own, and that people seemed to have to stay there until they were allowed to leave. I probably shouldn't have, but I told him about some of the crazy shit people would say in there, and how they seemed compelled to speak sometimes.

I told him that it all freaked me out sometimes, but that at the end of the day, we were getting high and fucked up in there all the time. So, we didn't really know what we saw and felt, and what we didn't.

He nodded along, and played with his rosary beads a little bit. He asked if we could pray when I pulled into the rectory to drop him off. I told him only if he kept his dress on.

"It's a cassock," he said with a sour face. It was clearly too early in our relationship for incessant priest abuse jokes.

Praying really seemed to make him feel better.

He prayed for guidance for us, his new friends in Christ, whatever that meant. He prayed for deliverance from demonic forces that plagued us. He prayed for safe passage for me.

He finished up and told me that it would really be best if he came back to the apartment sometime and blessed it. And he said not to talk to any presence we might encounter. I assured him that the Sky Lizard does all our negotiating, which drew a puzzled look from the good padre, a puzzled look he still had on his face as I pulled away and cracked my second beer.

I couldn't remember if I had told him about the Sky Lizard, and maybe that was why he looked confused. Or maybe he just hadn't realized until now that his responsible initiative of not drinking and driving had caused him to make one of his newfound flock drink and drive.

I figured next time I saw him I should tell him not to worry. I drink and drive all the time, with or without his help.

I was drinking again on the day of DooWop's funeral, although I wasn't driving. We had decided to walk in the procession. Chicago Shelly wanted to bring the procession down from St. Julian's, through the center of town, and out to the little cemetery on Butternut Hill. Saul and Jesus had converted two stolen shopping carts into a wheeled base for the little coffin to ride on. Katie and Randy had decorated it with some black velvet upholstery material and long black satin ribbons that trailed behind and added a certain somber ambience to the whole procession. Between that and the wailing mother and family it was quite a show.

We set out, that fine spring morning, birds chirping, dogwoods in bloom, high as hell, pushing a homemade hearse, on the way to bury a friend.

I had known other people to get killed, of course. But not anyone as integral to the group as DooWop had become. And Fr. Timothy's sermon at the funeral didn't help. He tried to make it into a celebration of life, and talked of how we'll all be reunited in heaven one day, etc.

But it just rang hollow, like the bells he played by pressing a little remote control he kept in the pocket of his dress.

"Don't even use hunchbacks no more, I guess," Randy had whispered. "Not even at funerals."

Chicago Shelly was holding things together

pretty well, considering she had just lost her son. Of course, Everett had gotten the oldest son killed in a similar fashion, and the middle daughter had run off and come back and run off and come back several times, so Chicago Shelly might have been getting used to losing children. She still had one boy in prison and the youngest boy with epilepsy, and the on again off again daughter, though.

Nobody talked to Everett at the funeral or the procession or the burial. Uncle Calvin stood with Shelly while Everett snuck off to smoke some of that shit he was always smoking, the shit that made him act the way he acted. Sometimes your dope can truly become who you are.

Boyd engaged Fr. Timothy in existentially the-ological conversation right away, which was good. Fr. Timothy looked like he could use some dis-traction. He had been crying up there during the Mass. I don't think he believed his sermon either. I chalked it up to him being a young priest and not yet used to the ways of the world. I figured a few more child funerals and he'd be old and craggy like the priests on TV.

"I'd like to come by your apartment and do a home blessing, if that's all right with you guys," he said as we ambled out of the cemetery and every-one began to go their separate ways. Randy had left a couple of minutes early to make it across town for Little Bro's meeting with the lawyer SSGT. Jones had found for him. The lawyer was a real slimy fucker out of Corbin, but he was a for-mer Marine so he had agreed to work on it pro bono. SSGT Jones was a convincing son of a bitch, after all.

"What does that entail, exactly?" Boyd asked, eyes narrowing in suspicion.

"Nothing much, really," Fr. Timothy said. He fumbled in his pocket and produced a little book, Minor Exorcisms, was printed in gold on the black leathery cover. The gold was faded, and the cover was well worn and cracked in places.

"I'll read a couple of prayers from this book and we'll work to free you all and the house from any-thing that is not of God."

I felt like we might be included in what is not of God, but I kept my mouth shut. No reason to antagonize him at this point, I figured. Boyd looked completely intrigued, but he said,

" I don't know Father; do you think it's neces-sary? We aren't demon possessed, are we? Wanna just send us home with some Holy Water and a Mary candle?"

Fr. Timothy made a face, and said,

"Boys, I've felt a lot of things over the years, and I definitely felt a presence at your apartment the other day. It could have been something else, or someone else not related to your apartment, but I think a home blessing is good for any home. And especially now, with the recent death of your friend, it is a good time to work on reconnecting with our Lord and Savior."

Katie hawked a lugee and spit it up into a dog-wood tree, the snot and spit smashing through several flowers before smacking into the trunk. Katie could spit almost 40 feet, if she wanted to, a skill I had never seen her use to such dramatic effect as she did just then to demonstrate her feelings about lords and saviors.

It startled Fr. Timothy, who began stammering about only if we wanted him to come over and such. Boyd placed his hand on his arm to calm him down, and spoke softly and sincerely.

"Of course, Padre, if you think it will help. Some of us are less attuned to workings of the spirit world than others, but we would be happy to indulge you," Boyd said with a calming smile.

"That's not exactly, I mean, it's not an indulgence exactly, and it's more for you than for me, I'm sorry, I shouldn't have brought it up," he fumbled through his feelings, clutching his rosary beads.

Katie rolled her eyes at me, but I said,

"No, no, Padre, we would love to have you over, and if an exorcism breaks out that will be okay too."

I didn't think it was possible for her to do, but Katie rolled her eyes in an even bigger roll than before, and spat even further up into another tree.

Fr. Timothy agreed to come over the next afternoon, and see what developed, and we agreed amongst ourselves that we wouldn't do anything to try and scare him, as funny as that would be. At least Boyd and I agreed, and we felt Randy would go along.

Katie was still spitting in trees on the walk home, to show her disgust with the idea of a priest coming over. Although she might have just been fucking with squirrels. It was hard to tell with her sometimes.

Eighteen

Father Timothy

The next morning, we knew we had a problem. The outlets in the kitchen all blew out at once in the middle of brewing coffee. I grabbed what little bit had made it through the percolation process and set out to find Saul. It was a Thursday, so I knew he was around early, trying to get a jump on Friday's work orders. He always started early on Thursday so he could get done early on Friday, which I felt was a good policy if you were bound by the typical conventions of the work week.

I, myself, prefer to take Thursdays and Fridays off. To get a jump on the weekend and all.

I found Saul repairing his wheelbarrow outside the maintenance garage. He used it as a personal garage sometimes too, it appeared, because there was an awful lot of shit in there that didn't have anything to do with apartment maintenance.

"I need some electrical help, Saul," I said, "if you're not too busy."

"I am always busy, you fucking gringo, why don't you get a job and then you can be busy too!" he said with a grin. Saul always liked to bust my balls, but in a good-natured type of way. He knew we never really asked him for anything unless it was really something that we didn't know how to fix ourselves.

Some tenants were whiny and needy and gave him shit for being Mexican, but we never did. He told me he would send Jesus over to take a look at it, directly, and went back to beating on his wheelbarrow with a hammer. Fixing it, some kind of way.

Jesus, it turned out, didn't really know shit about electricity either, but he was willing to learn.

First thing we learned is that he should shut the power off to the outlets he was working on.

Luckily, it was just a little zap, and he didn't let it faze him. Some men get scared after a little shock, but Jesus carried on, after flipping the kitchen breakers of course.

I moved the coffee pot into the living room so that we could carry on with the day. We made preparations for Fr. Timothy's visit, which consisted of cleaning up a little bit and smoking some pot to calm our nerves.

"Now don't act crazy when he's here, goddamit, just let him do his thing if it makes him feel better," Boyd instructed us as we passed the joint. Randy harrumphed and started flipping through his albums to find some mood music. He settled on Season of the Witch, which greeted Fr. Timothy as he came in.

"Thanks for having me over," he said as he greeted each of us.

Katie didn't look like she was happy about it, but she was behaving at least. We started off with some small talk, how long we had lived there, how we all got there, etc. Fr. Timothy looked uncomfortable when Boyd told him how his dad had almost killed him numerous times and how his mom thought it was best if he moved out for his senior year in high school.

And he looked sad when Randy told him about how his mother had passed and his dad had gotten lost in a bottle and how he felt that he and Little Bro needed a change, but now that seemed like a mistake, on account of Little Bro being brought up on murder charges.

And Fr. Timothy got downright squirmy when Randy relayed Katie's story, even though he edited it a lot, only mentioning that she had an abusive brother and mother and no father and had been on the streets for a while.

Fr. Timothy seemed relieved that I was only kicked out for being 18 and a drug addict.

Boyd asked him how he ended up in Bell County, and things got interesting. I don't think he meant to go into such detail, he definitely didn't plan it. But the Waiting Room would do that to you.

He started talking about his upbringing, rich family in Louisville, distillery folk, which is almost as good as horse folk, as far as folk go in Kentucky. They had maids and servants, lived on a large estate that had been in the family for generations. Several of the maids and servants lived in the slave quarters, but they had been updated in the '80s and weren't called slave quarters anymore.

"There are also salaries for the servants these days, good salaries for some of the more valuable ones," he said without a hint of irony, not realizing how that might sound to a non-slave owning person. But he continued,

"I was supposed to take over the family business, my daddy always said I had a good head for it, but that's just because my brother is a drunk and a womanizer and Daddy is afraid he will end up with bastard children that will encroach on the inheritance. Daddy is very concerned about bastard children and inheritance," he said with a faraway look in his eye.

I lit another joint and settled in for the rest of his story. Fascinating, to watch the upper crust delve into the depths of their well-funded psychosis. I always wondered if they would see the douchebaggery for what it was? Even if they didn't realize that the root of their problems was their dependence on and life consuming search for wealth, it still made for fascinating viewing.

"I went to boarding school up north, to learn proper mannerisms and prepare me for business school. I was supposed to go to Harvard, but I found myself drawn to the seminary. I couldn't shake this feeling that I was supposed to be doing something more with my life than selling bourbon," he said absently accepting the joint from Randy and passing it to Boyd without hitting it. At least he was participating in the passing, and I hoped we'd get him participating in the smoking next time around. At least he would smell like the sheep.

"My father was crushed, but my mother always wanted a priest in the family. And honestly, my sister is the one with the true head for business. Daddy always said it wasn't right for a woman to be in charge, but with only my brother left, he decided to let my sister have control. Besides, he started to really go with the Alzheimer's and she would have taken over anyway. My brother is a drunk and a nincompoop."

He'd had a revelation at seminary, he said, about how he wanted to help the poor, especially in Africa, and had even gone on a mission trip there, but he wasn't accepted into the program he wanted, because he was too newly ordained, so they sent him back to Kentucky to help us poor people here.

"Well, we are what they call a poverty pocket, Padre, and could probably use the help, as a region" Boyd tried to console him as he looked on the verge of tears thinking about how the bureaucracy was cheating him out of service to his God.

"But there was a woman," Fr. Timothy said, his voice beginning to shake. Katie glanced sharply in my direction, perking up to hear this new twist. She produced a joint and lit it up, handing it to the young priest as he began his tale.

"She was a parishioner at the church where I did my internship. Right after seminary they send you to be an associate at one of the big churches, the cathedral if there is room, but since the cathedral was full, I was sent to the big church, St. Peter and Paul, in downtown Lexington.

"I think I fell in love," he said looking at the joint burning in his hand, thinking about hitting it.

He passed it to Randy and continued,

"She had just had a tragedy in her life, her daughter had just died. The son pushed her down a well, as a prank, and she broke her neck and died. The husband had taken the cover off the well the day before to assess it or something, and had left the cover off. The little boy said he was just playing and thought it would be funny to push his sister in the hole."

"Jesus," I said.

"That's right, that's who I thought could help. Jesus," Fr. Timothy was staring into space again. Jesus stuck his head around the corner, saw us sitting there in the living room smoking dope with a priest, and ducked back into the kitchen.

"It started off with late night prayer sessions at the rectory. We would talk and pray, and drink wine. Always too much wine. She was so sad, but I began to see that when we were together, she started smiling here and there. We started watching movies every Thursday night, after the Spanish Mass. At first, they were religious documentaries, but it turned into romantic comedies and ended up love stories, sad ones about unrequited love and star-crossed lovers and the like."

He was fully chiefing on the joint every time it passed him now, as the Room started to get good to him. Boyd was twisting up another as we were finishing that one up. Randy had Led Zeppelin playing softly in the background, interspersed with Bob Dylan and Velvet Underground.

Fr. Timothy continued,

"I realized I was in trouble when I rented an apartment outside of town. My mother arranged it for me, I told her I needed somewhere private that I could pray and contemplate, away from the hustle and bustle of the rectory. Of course, it had to be kept secret. I gave a key to my special friend, just in case she came over for movie night and I wasn't there yet. No good having her sitting in the parking lot, we figured."

Boyd was starting to look concerned, slightly worried about what the priest was going to reveal next. I realized he actually liked the young priest and was feeling a little badly about the effect the Room was having on him.

But Fr. Timothy wasn't done yet. He had fully immersed himself in the Waiting Room experience and was just there, letting his story come out. I suppose in some ways we all need that outlet, that place to be able to let anything come out, to truly just let it all go.

The padre continued letting it go,

"She came over, just like I hoped she would, before I got there one particular Thursday. While I had been at Mass, she had been preparing the apartment. There were flowers in the vase by the door, a gentle breeze was blowing through carrying the fragrance from the candles she had lit, lavender and lilac.

"When I saw her, I knew I had screwed up. She was reclining on the couch, a glass of wine in one hand. She was in a very slinky dress, red like the rose petals that were strewn all over the floor. I knew I should leave, but she was too enticing. I came across the room and she stood up to meet me, grabbing me in a warm embrace. Our lips met and I saw heaven."

He paused and wiped a tear from his eye, before continuing,

"And I knew I was not supposed to see it in that way. She is married. I am a priest. I pulled away from her and ran. I ran to my car, drove to the rectory, busted in on the Monsignor and told him I had to go to Appalachia. I had to get out of this city of affluent horse farms and distilleries and get out into the hinterland to be with the people of God. And a week later I was here."

"What did you tell the lady?" Randy asked.

"Nothing. Nothing at all. I just left and haven't been able to bring myself to even contact her. And now I'm so afraid, and alone, and worried that someone will find out."

It was at about this time that he realized that several someone's had just found out, and he leaped up from the couch.

"Oh my God! What have I done?" he called out, frantically searching for his hat and leaping over the coffee table as he tried to escape.

Boyd tried to call out after him that we were good at keeping our mouths shut, that the Room happened to everyone, that it was ok and Jesus still loved him, but it was no use. He burst out the door, leaving it standing open, and ran down the steps two at a time, a wild and frantic look on his face.

He rushed right past two rough looking hombres, who were coming up the stairs in search of their quarry. They had been on the hunt for some time, and Francisco, the leader, was growing tired of this assignment. They were looking for a man who had killed their boss's son.

The son was an idiot, and probably deserved it,

and Francisco had thought many times about re-moving the son himself. He had cursed the son's dead soul just that morning when he had endured the racist taunts of the gas station clerk outside Knoxville when they stopped to fuel up and get some grub.

The clerk had called him "Chief," he assumed because he was from Mexico but to the dumb gringo he looked like an Apache. Francisco was ready to end this business and return home, just as soon as they found this fucking Ecuadorian asshole who killed the boss's idiot son.

He paused and watched the priest running from the apartment on the second floor. The apartment he was heading to. The apartment that Ecuadorian bastard had been seen walking into just an hour or so before.

"Que?" his partner, Eduardo asked.

Eduardo would have preferred to wait in the car, but Rodrigo had been insistent that it was his turn to wait in the car. So Eduardo had reluctantly racked a round into the chamber of his 9mm and followed Francisco up the stairs. And now, Francisco was stopping in the middle of the staircase like an asshole.

"Nothing, amigo. Just some crazy gringo priest. Let's go," Francisco assured him, and they continued up the stairs, headed toward the Waiting Room.

Nineteen

Francisco

Francisco was tired. He hated the USA, fucking gringos everywhere. They had been on the trail of this Ecuadorian bastard for months. They had lost him in Oklahoma for a few weeks, until that waitress opened up to Eduardo.

She had seen the Ecuadorian get into a semi with Arkansas plates headed east on I-40. They had followed the trail to Memphis, where they missed him by two days. The Ecuadorian had apparently been stabbed in a barfight and stayed holed up in the back of a grocery store while he healed.

The store owner hadn't wanted to talk, himself being from Ecuador. Trying to look out for his countryman, Francisco figured. That kind of nationalistic pride will get you fucked up in Francisco's world, as the grocer had learned. He still had eight toes, and his wife still had one eye.

Fucking Ecuadorians. Worse than the Nicaraguans, in Francisco's opinion. Still seemed wild, fucking jungle people, at least in Francisco's limited experience. To be honest, he sometimes shot before he questioned them.

But this fucking Ecuadorian. There would be questioning. And torture. That's why he had brought Eduardo. Eduardo was head of his class at the university, before the cartel pulled him out. Burned the school down actually, but that's only what the intelligentsia truly deserved. In Francisco's opinion.

In any case, Eduardo was a valuable asset, he could keep a victim alive for days. And they were going to need this Ecuadorian asshole alive when they got back to Mexico. Don Pedro wanted some time with him.

As his snakeskin boots brought him step by step closer to the Waiting Room's door, which was still ajar from the fleeing priest, Francisco had an overwhelming feeling of dread, an utterly mystifying notion to turn back. He paused for just a moment, curious about this premonition, this peculiar feeling.

But being Francisco, dreaded enforcer of the Catalina Cartel, he pushed forward. He pushed the door to the apartment slowly open the rest of the way with the barrel of his nickel plated .10mm he loved so much.

The door swung open to reveal only darkness. There did not appear to be any light on in the apartment, save a dull red glow emanating from the darkest recesses of the deepest bowels of the place.

Eduardo drew his breath sharply as he passed through the doorway, slowly following Francisco, who was slowly following that nickel plated .10mm down the hallway. Francisco could hear music wafting toward him from the source of the red light, joined by the marijuana smoke that was swirling in clouds that twisted and danced on their way down the hallway to the open doorway.

It was hot in here, Francisco decided as he made his way carefully down the hall. He was sweating, and he could hear Eduardo behind him, mopping the sweat from his face and almost whimpering.

Fucking Eduardo, always whining, he thought. Still no sound of people, only the music playing softly on the radio, something about Sweet Jane.

As he came to the end of the hall, he paused for a second at the corner of the wall, realizing the room was opening out in front of him. There was only darkness to the left, with the incandescent light from inside a room making an outline of a doorway. Probably a bathroom or a bedroom.

The red light was coming from the room directly in front of him, with the music generating its creepy melody from somewhere off to the right side in the room. He felt Eduardo in his back, and took a step forward, his gun moving just past the corner of the wall as he tried to make out the dim shapes shrouded in darkness.

This fucking red light, he thought.

Randy saw them first, when they breached the doorway that Fr. Timothy had so impolitely left vulnerable. Randy had been seated on the couch under the Last Supper, only way down there at the Bartholomew end, where he could see down the hallway. He had quickly and quietly slumped down into the couch, trying his best to not afford the intruders any semblance of an outline.

You must be the lumpy pillows, Randy always said.

From his vantage point he watched Francisco and Eduardo slowly make their way down the hallway as the Velvet Underground serenaded them. Randy had given us sleight hand signals to let us know there were two intruders, and they had guns.

Boyd had maneuvered over to the corner where the hallway and the Waiting Room proper met and was pressed flat against the wall, just waiting for them to make it down to him.

I was set up in the corner opposite the entrance, where I could fire without hitting Boyd if I was careful with my angles. Assuming they made it past Boyd and actually out into the room.

Katie was in the bathroom, the light making a perfect rectangle around the door. I wasn't worried about her; she knew to take cover once the shooting starts.

It was all going according to plan, when Jesus threw a curveball into the whole thing. It wasn't really his fault. Jesus didn't know what was going on, and at the moment Francisco's nickel plated .10mm made its way past the edge of the corner, Jesus flipped the breaker and the kitchen lights roared to life.

Francisco paused for just a second, and looked with squinting eyes toward the kitchen and the newfound light illuminating the scene. He missed the light glinting off the blade of Boyd's Katana as it came down with an ominous whish, severing Francisco's hand and the pistol it gripped.

Francisco, clearly shocked at the turn of events, screamed like a banshee, holding his bloody stump up to his face, not believing what he saw. Eduardo was frozen in place, stammering, in Spanish,

"The Ecuadorian, donde esta the penche Ecuadorian?"

At this point, Katie burst from the bathroom, flinging the door open and bathing Francisco and Eduardo in the full complement of 150 watts of incandescent filament, provided by the 4 vanity bulbs she had just upgraded so she could pluck her eyebrows with ease. She said one couldn't really see with those damn CFL bulbs they were pushing at the Wal-Mart.

Katie screamed at the intruders, in perfect

Spanish, as near as I could tell from my two years of high school espanol,

"This is Hell's Waiting Room! No one may leave until they have been called! You are intruding and will suffer the wrath of El Diablo!"

Eduardo dropped his gun and ran, screaming, from the apartment, down the stairs, and into the safety of the car. I wasn't sure, but I think he beat Father Timothy's time.

Francisco, on the other hand, was still in shock. But he was somehow able to grasp what was happening. He looked down at his hand on the ground, and started to bend over, but Katie growled,

"Leave it, and go!"

Francisco straightened back up, set his jaw in determination, nodded toward Jesus, who was peeking through the kitchen doorway, shock and awe in his eyes, and said,

"What about him? I must have him for the jeffe. Otherwise I cannot return to Mexico."

Katie repeated,

"No one may leave until they have been called!"

"You should really go get that bandaged, any-way" I offered by way of compromise.

Francisco nodded, glared one more time at Jesus, spun on his heel and marched out of the apartment, muttering about bad juju and the boss's idiot dead son.

Boyd followed him down the hallway, switching to his pistol to cover him in such a tight space and locking the door behind the swearing Mexican.

"That was fuckin trippy!" Randy exclaimed, materializing out of the couch where he had, in fact, been the lumpy pillows.

"That was A-one, top of the line, you ain't never seen no shit like this before, trippy." He was grinning ear to ear as he picked up Francisco's hand to examine the cut.

"Fucking clean. What do you wanna do with this?" he asked.

"Wrap that in plastic and stick it in the freezer, I guess. Fuck, what are we going to do, Jack?" Boyd said, like I had any ideas whatsoever.

"I don't know, man. Cutting off a Mexican's hand with a sword was not on my to do list for today, so I really don't know where to go from here. What about him?"

I gestured toward Jesus, who was deep in prayer

to the Virgin Mary it looked like, kneeling in front of Katie as she held his hands.

"And how long have you known Spanish?" I asked, heading to the fridge to get a beer. Fuck I needed more than a beer at this point.

Randy was wrapping the hand with saran wrap, and using too much if we're being honest. Does freezer burn really matter on a severed hand? It was still clutching the gun, which was making the wrapping more difficult, I suppose.

Rather than offer any help, I went to the window to see if they were mounting a full assault out there.

"What are they doing? Are they still there?" Boyd asked as he joined me at the window with a Xanax and a joint.

"For the head," he said, handing me the pill while he lit the joint.

"From what I can tell, the little one is cauterizing the big one's stump with a blowtorch and a piece of iron. Think they're in it for the long haul?" I asked, not even really sure what the long haul was.

"Anybody that carries a blow torch with them just in case they need to cauterize a stump is in it for the long haul, my friend. We just have to figure out how to deal with them, I suppose. Let's start with the Mexican in the kitchen," Boyd answered.

"I think he's from Ecuador," I offered weakly.

It was turning into a fucked-up day.

Twenty

Our Witch Is No Match for Their Witch

We found Jesus kneeling in front of the Last Supper Tapestry with the High Voltage sticker over Jesus's face. He was deep in prayer as Katie looked on in wonder.

We had left Randy at the window to watch the medical proceedings in the parking lot. From his narration, it sounded as if they had gotten Francisco bandaged up and he was resting comfortably in the backseat. Randy told us,

"the other one, who didn't come up here with

Capt. Hook and Smee is sitting in the front seat of the long black Lincoln smoking cigarettes and watching."

"Watching, watching, all watching. Us. Hell's Waiting Room," Randy hummed to the tune of the Sky Lizard's Anthem.

Periodically, the other one, who didn't come up here, would say a little prayer, make the sign of the cross, kiss his Rosary beads he was clutching, and do a little bow. Randy seemed to feel, as far as I could tell from the narration, which seemed to wander quite a bit after Katie passed out another round of Xanax to help us calm down, that 'the one who didn't come up here' had religion in some sort of way, and was probably praying for our immediate demise and, Randy wanted to know, how did we feel about that?

"What the fuck's going on, man?" Boyd demanded of Jesus, interrupting his prayer time. Katie shot Boyd a look, clearly disappointed that he had ruined whatever trip she was watching unfold through truthful, contrite prayer in the Waiting Room. It was the first time anybody had prayed that hard in there.

I was a little curious if it would work, myself.

We heard a knock on the door. It was at this point that I realized Randy's narration was on tape delay and was running several minutes behind. As Boyd went to see who was at the door, Randy was saying,

"Now Captain Hook is waving Saul over, but he doesn't have a hand, so he just looks like he's waving his bloody stump in defeat. But Smee is also waving him over now. They're pointing and gesturing up here. And the religious one is making the sign of the cross, a lot, and it seems very important that Saul know what is happening up here. And I think they might be telling him to come up here and talk to us. He's on his way up here. Probably to talk to us. Smee is smoking another cigarette. Captain Hook is laying down again. I think Saul will be here soon."

Meanwhile, Saul was explaining to Boyd, from the doorway, that he didn't want to even be involved this much, and that there was no way he was coming inside to talk.

"And they say to tell you they only want Jesus. They don't want any bad juju from you or this Casa de Diablo, and they want you to keep your Witch inside, but please, they must have Jesus so they can return to their master. Boss. Jeffe. They said to tell you they will wait outside for you to release Jesus from your grasp, and they will not come inside, they will leave in peace. Except for Jesus. For him there will be much horribleness. But you they will not harm, if you release Jesus to them. But they have called for their own Witch Doctor. And when he arrives, he will vanquish your Witch, and then they will come inside to retrieve Francisco's hand, and Jesus, and then to kill all of you."

Randy emerged from his observation post by the bedroom window in time to say,

"Saul, what are you doing here?" and wink at Boyd and me, secure in the knowledge that Saul had no idea he had been under surveillance. Saul looked blankly at him, nodded to Boyd, and beat a hasty retreat back down the stairs.

Boyd closed the door, repeating quietly to himself,

"their own witch doctor, Their own witch doctor, their Own witch doctor, their own Witch doctor, their own witch Doctor."

Finally he concluded, as he sat down on the couch and contemplated Jesus, who was still deep in prayer,

"Doesn't matter how you place the emphasis on it; we might be fucked."

I figured Boyd would know, himself having a witch doctor in the family, his great Uncle Mat. Mat was dead and gone before I ever came around Boyd's family, but the stories of hexes and curses and spells were slightly terrifying. And it wasn't just Boyd telling ghost stories to scare us while we were high. If Mat was a hoax, the whole damn family and half the holler were in on it, cause they all backed up the stories.

But he was dead now, and we didn't really know any other witch doctors. Randy was a little concerned that Katie was our witch, but we assured him it was just a misunderstanding, we did not in fact have our own witch. Randy did not look entirely convinced, however.

We were apparently going to need a witch when the Cartel's witch doctor got here to do battle. What the fuck to do?

We set about working on thinking about trying to come up with a plan. The first step, as always, was to smoke some pot.

"What if..." Randy began, and then trailed off. He had done this several times already, and I generally paid his initial what if's very little attention. He eventually continued,

"But what if we just gave them Jesus? Maybe they deserve to catch him. Maybe he was jacking off in their apartments too. Maybe he did God knows what, and we are standing in the way of justice?"

"Does it feel like we're standing in the way of justice?" I asked, honestly thinking about it myself.

"No," Randy said.

"And what would DooWop say?" Boyd asked.

"Jesus did save DooWop and Little Bro that time," he added, as Katie nodded along with him.

"Yeah, you're right," Randy answered.

"But what the fuck are we going to do? Their gonna bring a whole hell of a lot more guys next time. What the fuck are we going to do?"

It was a true conundrum. In a cosmic way, we owed it to DooWop to defend his defender, and in a cosmic way, fuck the Mexican drug cartel, and in a cosmic way, we really needed a witch or something if that was the way they wanted to play this thing.

Otherwise, we were going to need a lot more firepower.

What we really probably needed was an escape plan.

Boyd had been sitting quietly, watching Jesus pray his various litanies and rosaries for the novena, and absently flicking a toggle switch back and forth. We had shoplifted the toggle switch from Walmart the other day to experiment with making a detonator. Boyd was still trying to come up with a senior project for graduation. He only had a few weeks left in his high school career, assuming he passed the senior project, and I had advised against building a bomb, even if it was presented as a science project.

But he was running short of time, and he really did like to blow shit up.

Randy had begun his project the other day, an artistic masterpiece showcasing the degradation and filth of society. He had cleared the coffee table of all the usual mess, beer cans, cigarette butts, food wrappers, etc., and placed a piece of poster board down on the top of the coffee table. This had been about a week ago. And as the days passed, the filth and garbage reaccumulated on the coffee table, this time with the poster board under it. His plan was to painstakingly glue each individual piece of trash in place on the poster board, then lift the poster board and all its glued trash out of the mess that was the coffee table, and bring his Ode to Filth in for his senior project. He was calling it "A Day in the Life."

Boyd was flicking the toggle switch, click, click, click, and one of those clicks flipped on a light bulb in his brain that almost jumped out of the top of his head like they do on cartoons. He jumped up like something crazy, grabbed a notebook and hopped up onto the back of the couch where he could sit eye level with the Sky Lizard. That's how I knew it was going to be a good plan, the Lizard was in on it.

"Randy, turn us on some contemplation music, Jack light us up another joint, Katie grab us a couple of beers. I've got a little something brewing that just might work!"

He called out directions like a tank commander, pointing and gesturing with his pen as he furiously scribbled in his notebook. Suddenly he flung the notebook across the room and into the corner by the speaker, jumped up and ran into the kitchen.

Into the kitchen, he ran, to retrieve the reserve

of cocaine from the stash that Fathead had left us, cocaine which is, of course, the heart and soul of any good scheme.

He began to explain his plan as he lined out the coke.

"It seems to me that the root of the problem is that the cartel wants Jesus. But if Jesus is dead, they should just return to Mexico, their mission completed in an unfortunate, but very definitive sort of way."

"So, we kill Jesus?" Randy asked, glancing over at Jesus to see if he was listening. He was, and was eyeing the door and thinking about whether it was more dangerous in here with the crazies or out there with the murderers.

"No, no, no," Boyd said as he came up off a line.

"We just make it look like he's dead. Fake his death."

Katie looked intrigued, and nestled into Boyd's shoulder, mostly so she could get at the dope mirror. I figured she should go next anyway, being the newly minted witch and all.

"We lure Tweeker Dave out of his apartment, have Dad help us make a little explosive charge that we have Saul plant in there while he pretends to do some maintenance. Jesus runs from here up to there, and lets the boys out front see him go in. He climbs out the kitchen window and over to Betty's kitchen window next door. We blow the charge, and they think Jesus has been blown up in an unfortunate meth lab accident. Easy peasy."

"Why Tweeker Dave?" I asked.

"Because nobody would believe he DIDN'T have a meth lab up there," Boyd said simply.

It made sense, really, in an absolutely fucked up, ridiculous, and crazy kind of way.

"You think Hippy John will be down to help us?" Randy questioned as he did his line. It was too big, it looked like, because he fell back into the couch with his eyes rolling back in his head and probably missed Boyd's answer.

"An excuse to blow shit up? In town? Hippy John will be all over that shit," Boyd had replied, setting us up for another round of coke.

"Now all we need is a dead Mexican."

I smiled as I sat back and enjoyed my buzz. It just might work, and what a fucking sendoff for Jesus! Jacking off little bastard that he was.

But as I sat there watching him pray in the corner near the notebook, I figured he might not be as excited about the plan as we were.

I knew it was no longer up to him, though.

As the Sky Lizard looked on, I realized it had never been up to Jesus. As soon as he entered the Waiting Room, he gave up that decision, just like the rest of us.

Twenty-One

Cocaine Complexities

The plan started to get complicated when the reinforcements arrived. A second Lincoln Continental pulled into the parking lot a couple of days later. Francisco had called for backup to help keep the place under 24-hour surveillance until the witch doctor arrived.

We made Saul engage Eduardo in conversation at the Taco truck while he was getting lunch for all of them. According to Saul, Eduardo said they now had six men, working shifts to cover the front and the back, and the witch doctor should be arriving in a week. Apparently, he was tied up on another case in Juarez, but should be finishing it up soon and headed our way.

We realized after the second day that we could come and go at our leisure, as far as the chollos were concerned. They were only there for Jesus and they thought we were protected by our witch, Katie, anyway. This afforded us the opportunity to put the rest of the plan into action.

First thing we had to do was get Hippy John on board.

"Why don't you just shoot 'em?" was his first question.

It did seem like we were going through a lot of trouble, admittedly, but we figured that shooting them would just cause more chollos to come looking into who shot their compadres.

"Well, I don't know if it's the best idea I ever heard, but I do like to blow shit up. When do you need it?" Hippy John said with that glimmer of crazy in his eye.

He agreed to bring the device by the apartment in two days so he could see the layout and show us where and how to set it up to destroy Tweeker Dave's apartment, without damaging anything else. We knew if anybody could pull that off it was Hippy John.

Big D came by to drop one problem on our laps, but ended up being the solution to one of our other problems. The problem he brought was Fathead's cocaine problem. He was still scared to sell any of it, and was holed up in his house and doing the kilo by himself. Big D was worried about him. It was Randy that thought of the solution.

"What if he sells it back to these Mexicans?" Randy asked. "They don't know no fucking bikers, man, so it won't get back to JT."

Big D glanced over at Jesus, who was in the midst of the Angelus prayers for noontime. We had set him up with a pallet in the corner where Boyd had chucked his notebook, and he had built a little shrine to Jesus and Mary out of candles and crucifixes and little statues that Katie kept bringing him from somewhere.

Fleetwood Mac Laura had been coming by as of late to pick her up for these religious trinkets shopping trips. The two of them were really becoming the best of friends, which made me smile. Katie could use a girlfriend, I thought.

"That might work, especially if we can coordinate with you and Fathead for the deal to take place on Monday afternoon so at least some of the Mexicans will be distracted," Boyd said, wheels turning in his mind.

It had been a source of consternation as to how to keep them from seeing Jesus climbing from one apartment to the other before the explosion. Maybe Big D and Fathead could at least occupy a few of them for a couple of hours.

Big D said it was worth a shot, anything to get Fathead out of the coke binge he was in. We had already contracted with Bev to take Tweeker Dave out for a date on Monday afternoon, so things looked to be falling into place.

"Now all we need is a body," Boyd said after Big D left. "Where the fuck are we going to find a dead Mexican?"

Randy looked over at Jesus, which made us all laugh, except Jesus, who prayed that much harder for deliverance from these crazy gringos and the cartel henchmen outside.

Twenty-Two

The Weekend

It was a problem. We were setting everything up for Monday, and still no body. It was already Thursday. Luckily, Margot came over on Thursdays pretty regularly, and on this particular Thursday she brought her pretty little sophomore friend, Emily. And Emily's dad owned the funeral home on Cumberland Avenue, Flannigan's Funeral Services. We were explaining the dilemma to them over a blunt they had brought and some margheritas I was mixing up, when Emily blurted out,

"I can get you a dead Mexican! My daddy was

talking all about it this morning at breakfast. He was talking to Scooter on the phone, who works the tow truck for the highway department, and they were pulling a U-Haul out of the ditch on Sugar Run Road. Scooter told him they would be by with about six or seven bodies for Daddy to clean up and get buried. Daddy loves those kinds of wrecks, cause the state pays by the head and there ain't much paperwork on account of they're illegals and don't have identifications. You could have one of them for your little project here. He's gonna charge the highway department for ten, whether you use one or not."

Somewhere in the conversation, Emily had lost track of if we were talking about Boyd's senior project explosion or the Save Jesus explosion, but we knew in the end it didn't really matter. What mattered was figuring out how to steal a body from the funeral home.

Emily promised to meet us there on Friday night with her Daddy's keys if we would let her help us. She just wanted to do something illegal and exciting, which was basically our M.O. for Margot's crowd of well-adjusted white kids. They were just slumming with the deadbeats and the criminals.

"It's a date," Boyd had said, and Emily had swooned. She had a major crush on Boyd, which would have led to other things had he not been so preoccupied with the current situation. He had a one-track mind when it came to explosions. He'd rather blow shit up than just about anything else. And a good scam operation was a close second.

Margot and Emily showed up right on time Friday night and we got in and out of the funeral home, no problem. We picked an approximate match out of the selection of dead bodies, although we thought Katie or someone would need to give this guy a haircut to make him look more like Jesus. But we figured if we put Jesus's maintenance uniform on him, nobody would be able to tell the difference after they pulled the body from the fire.

We had been preparing for the body's arrival by having Randy run a bunch of errands, in and out of the apartment all day wearing a bright orange Tennessee Vols jacket and his plain black cap. It was a little warm for a jacket, but we needed the cartel watchers to observe him in that outfit so we could put the body in it to walk up the stairs.

Boyd and I did the three-legged race deal to get him up the stairs. Randy had gone to stay at his dad's for the night, and they were meeting up with SSGT Jones and the lawyer for Little Bro early the next morning after church. Randy's dad, despite being a drunk and a fuckup always dragged the boys to church if they were around. Probably figured having the kids with him helped his widower sympathy card he would undoubtedly play on the congregation.

After we got the body into the apartment, we realized somebody better explain to Jesus what was going on. He looked a little freaked out when we came dragging a fresh Mexican body into the place.

Katie explained it all to him, emphasizing that while we knew he was from Ecuador, and this dead gentleman might be of Mexican origin, to the redneck EMT's and police in Middlesboro, it was all the same. And the official report would reflect that the unidentified maintenance man was in fact killed in the explosion in Tweeker Dave's apartment, and that would be enough to convince the cartel that he was dead.

Jesus didn't look entirely convinced, but he seemed to perk up a little bit at the prospect of weaseling his way out of this pickle.

Fathead showed up Saturday afternoon with a bit of good news as well. He had met the cartel guys through Saul, and they had agreed to take the cocaine off his hands. Rock bottom prices, but he would be rid of it. He brought an ounce of it over to celebrate his impending sale.

We figured we were lucky he brought it over beforehand, in case they just killed him and took it, but we didn't want to spoil the mood so no one brought that scenario up. You could tell Randy really wanted to, though.

"Big D told me about your plan, dog," Fathead said as the party tray passed around the room. He continued,

"And I think we could do even better. I met those guys over at the pool hall where they were having a drink in between their shifts out here in the parking lot. And what if Big D gets them into a long-term pool hustle, drag the games out forever, keeping them on the line thinking they can win their money back, but making it take forever, you know, to buy you more time?"

"Yeah, I could do that," Big D offered.

"It'll be kind of fun. And maybe I can win all the money they talked out of Fathead's cocaine price," he said with a laugh, as Fathead glared at him.

We all agreed Fathead was getting hosed a little bit, but that Big D keeping them occupied as long as possible was definitely a good thing. It was at this moment that Hippy John showed up with the pyrotechnics.

Nobody remembered that he was going to stop by, otherwise we would have hidden the coke.

"Well holy shit fire, what the fuck is going on in here?!" he exclaimed upon entering the Waiting Room.

"Don't mind if I do!" he said pleasantly when Katie offered him the party tray with line after line of beautifully manicured cocaine. Hippy John took one to each nostril and let out a

"Pheeeeewwwww," as if the weight of the world had been lifted off his shoulders. Surprise cocaine is always the best cocaine.

I was smoking a cigarette and Hippy John

bounced over and plopped down on the couch next to me.

"Twist us up a doofus, Jacko, and I'll show you how this little firecracker operates," he said, grooving to the Grateful Dead Randy had going on the jukebox. He produced a cigar box from his bag as I produced a paper from my pack and Katie handed me the pot. Hippy John flipped open the cigar box with a flourish.

"Now this here timer can be set for two-minute increments. You'll probably need at least 4 minutes to make sure you are clear of the room and out of the apartment. Is it set up like this one?" he asked, surveying the apartment from the couch. I nodded, and he continued,

"You should put it back there in the kitchen, maybe on the counter so it will be in the approximate location of a meth setup. Now I've included some of J-Rod's bathtub meth sprinkled all in so they can find some residue, but that might not matter because this homemade napalm is gonna throw all over the room and completely disfigure yore Mexican if you prop him up next to it."

"Is that big enough?" I asked.

"We need it to blow up the body pretty good

to help with the identification process. Or lack thereof. The napalm is a nice touch, and I guess you're right, they won't be able to I.D. shit anyway."

"Son, this is my own ANFO mixture with a little telluride, and of course, a few personally manufactured ingredients. It will absolutely destroy that kitchen up there, but it won't do much damage besides that, blast will go mostly up. You put that body in there in the kitchen with it, though, and you'll have pieces all the way out here in the living room."

Hippy John leaned back on the couch under the Lord's Supper and said,

"Boys, y'all have got to trust me. I'm a professional."

We were in no position to argue, and it was too late to come up with another blasting plan anyway. Besides, I did trust Hippy John when it came to this shit. Hippy John had been a blaster down at the mines for years. As he put it one time,

"Boys, I've blowed shit up in them mines for years and ain't caved one in yet!"

You couldn't trust him around cocaine, though, which became apparent soon enough. Fathead and Big D left, and Boyd hid the bulk of our cocaine while Randy distracted Hippy John with some live Queen records. Hippy John loved him some Queen.

Satisfied that he had done up all the cocaine in the apartment, and eventually convinced that none of us knew how to get ahold of Fathead, that bastard who had run off with the main stash, and finally agreeing that we were not going to go with him on a fruitless search for more cocaine, Hippy John bid us all adieu.

"Two-minute increments, Dumbass!" he called as he headed toward the door, admonishing us in the most fatherly of ways to be careful lest we blow ourselves up.

It was good advice, I thought later, as I lay in bed trying to smoke enough pot to fall asleep. Don't blow ourselves up. Good advice indeed.

Twenty-Three

Sunday Funday

We had the bomb, we had the Big D pool hustle distraction, and we had contingency plans for everything else in motion. Betty had agreed to hold a BBQ out front to get everyone out of the building, using a giant pack of hotdogs and a couple of family packs of hamburger that Randy had pilfered from the Piggly Wiggly.

Saul had agreed to cut the gas to the building at our signal so that maybe we really wouldn't blow everything all the way up.

We had Bev keeping Tweeker Dave out of his apartment for a few hours.

Margot was coming over with a couple of scantily clad friends to stage a carwash in the parking lot of the consignment store that faced the back of our building, to occupy the one guy left to watch for Jesus back there. Figured his Lincoln could use a wash, and Margot could distract a man or two if she put her mind to it.

But we still didn't have a good way to get the body upstairs into Tweeker Dave's apartment.

We had been getting high all day, trying to think of a solution, when Randy spoke up. He had just returned from the meeting with SSGT Jones and the lawyer. They were feeling good about Little Bro's chances of avoiding heavy jail time, so Randy was in good spirits.

"Well, you're always going to have problems moving a body in one piece. What if we cut it up in the tub, and then carry it up there in backpacks or something?" he asked.

Katie gagged a little bit, and spit a huge lugee across the room, through the open bathroom door and into the sink. It was a nice shot.

"That's interesting," Boyd mumbled, getting up

from the couch and examining the dead Mexican we had sat in the corner. Katie had given him a haircut and we had a full set of Maintenance clothes on him that Saul had provided.

"I guess we would hack him up in the clothes, so the body parts will look like they were clothed when they blew up?" he asked no one in particular.

It sounded reasonable to me, so I helped Randy carry the body into the bathroom and we placed it in the tub. Boyd and Katie were busily gathering swords and cleavers and saws, all the other standard tools for dismembering a body.

We decided we better smoke some pot before we got too involved in the hacking up process. I thought the anti-nausea properties of marijuana would help the situation, but it was too little too late. Randy had looked queasy when we were moving the body into the tub.

And high or not, when I held the arm up so that Boyd could take a swing at it with his sword, Randy lost his lunch. He was holding the foot, I suppose so the body couldn't run away, and as Boyd began to swing the Katana toward the outstretched arm, aiming just inside the shoulder,

Randy blew chunks all over the foot he was hold-ing, all over the arm I was holding, all over the sword and all over Boyd and all over the tub and all over the rest of the body and all over absolutely everything.

Once he got started there was no holding back, and pretty quickly the entire bathroom seemed to be covered with Randy's puke. Which made Boyd start puking, because anybody else puking always made Boyd puke.

I released the arm, which had only received a glancing blow anyway, and jumped back out of the room, covered in vomit. Katie was doubled over with laughter in the hallway. I told her it wasn't funny, as I was starting to laugh myself.

Boyd emerged next, and when I saw him, I re-alized I was not actually covered in vomit, I was in fact only lightly sprayed. Boyd was covered in vomit. He did not think it was funny in the least, and he made a sour face every time we heard Randy wretch and heave, still in the bathroom.

"This is fucked," was all Boyd said, which set Katie and me off again.

We heard Randy turn the shower on, still heav-ing and coughing and spitting, and I smoked a cigarette while watching him through the doorway. He was trying his best to hose everything down with the shower, including the body which was now covered in his DNA, and Boyd's DNA. It was a comical sight, but I figured I better get in there and help him wash away as much evidence as we could.

A few hours later we had the body washed down, the maintenance uniform removed, laundered, and replaced, the bathroom cleaned, our puke clothes laundered, we were all freshly showered and we only had one problem.

"We're out of beer," Randy said.

Ok, two problems. We also still had to figure out how to get the body upstairs to Tweeker Dave's apartment. And we needed beer. Boyd and I decided to go on the beer run, and we hoped that by stepping away from the dead body situation for a minute we would be able to think of a solution.

The only place we could get booze in those days, operating as we were without a fake ID, and liquor stores being closed on Sundays anyways, was the bootlegger out in Frakes. It was about a 45-minute drive from the apartment, one-way, so we figured that would give us plenty of time to sort things out.

All we knew for sure was that we were doing the right thing, trying to save Jesus. We weren't entirely sure if he deserved what the chollos had planned for him, but based on having saved DooWop and Little Bro, we figured he had earned some goodwill on the karmic level.

"I mean, he seems like maybe he's a creeper, based on the Phantom Jackoff move in Bev's apartment, but he did rescue our boys," Boyd had said.

I agreed, although we were no closer to a plan to move the body when we pulled off the main road at the Wasioto Winds golf course to follow the two-lane road up into the holler. It was late, after dark, and the golf course was closed, but we saw a figure walking along their parking lot fence, carrying what appeared to be a baseball bat.

"Didn't they take the batting cages out last summer?" I asked.

"Yeah, so what in the fuck is this guy doing. Holy shit! Slow down, I think it's Jimbo!" Boyd exclaimed, calling out the window as I pulled over,

"Hey! Jimbo!"

Jimbo turned around when he heard his name.

It was in fact him and he did in fact have a baseball bat. He broke into a big toothy grin when he saw Boyd, his great mountain man beard parting like the Red Sea to reveal his pearly whites.

"Boys am I glad to see you!" he said as he hurried up to the car.

"Like my new ball bat?" he asked with a smile.

"Absolutely, Jimbo, where did you get it?" Boyd asked, knowing there would be a story.

"Hop in and tell us about it," I said.

"Took it off these two knuckleheads that tried to jump me a little bit ago. I was just walking, right? And they tried to come at me with this bat. They got me good with the first lick, but you know it takes more than a ball bat to bring me down! I took it off that boy and beat his brains out with it. The other one run off before I could get to him, but I'll find him. What are you boys up to?"

I had pulled back out onto the road while Jimbo related his story. We still needed alcohol, after all. So I said,

"We're headed up here to get some beer, then probably back home. We got a big day tomorrow."

"Well, Boys," Jimbo said with a smile that even I could see from the front seat,

"This here ball bat ain't all I've got this evening," and he pulled back his coat to reveal the single biggest Mason jar I had ever seen. It looked like one of those pickled egg jars they have in redneck gas stations, it was so fucking big. And it was filled almost to the top with a crystal-clear liquid: white lightning, grade a, top shelf moonshine.

"This here is the best I've ever tasted," Jimbo said with a smile.

"Care for a snort, Boyd?"

Boyd did in fact care for a snort, as did I, as did we all. Good moonshine is one of the best booze buzzes you can get, and Jimbo always had a good connection.

The last thing I remember is Boyd saying,

"Maybe just the one, Jimbo, cause Jack is right. We got a big day tomorrow, and a few more preparations to make tonight."

I don't remember going into the bootlegger's den, although, apparently I did, based on all the beer cans I found in the car when I woke up.

I was alone in the car and it was parked under a tree in a field up behind what appeared to be a dairy barn. The couple of cows I saw wandering didn't seem to be wondering about me, so I figured this was an authorized parking spot.

I climbed out of the backseat, which made me wonder who had been driving, and stumbled toward the dairy barn, which looked less and less like a dairy barn the closer I got to it. I realized there were other people milling about, both outside and inside the barn.

And there didn't seem to be any animals actually here in the barn, it was actually quite clean and swept up. For a barn. And there were an inordinate number of young women lazing about, with hollow eyes and glazed expressions on their faces.

One pretty little redhead came up to me, grabbed my hand, and said,

"You got time for a good time, loverboy?"

I answered that for her I had all the time in the world, but no cash, and had she seen my friend Boyd around anywhere.

She withdrew her hand with a disgusted look on her face, and used it to point up the staircase, which led to the transactional portion of the facility.

I found Boyd, naked, face down on a grimy mattress in the corner of a room that was serving a party of at least four. The other patrons seemed unconcerned with my entering and unconcerned with Boyd having been in there.

He mumbled hello, as I helped him find his clothes, and I dragged him down the stairs. The sign on the door said "Now leaving the Doo Drop Inn" and the double oo's in Doo had nipples drawn on them. The redhead waved as we made our way to the VIP lot, apparently having gotten over her disgust at my financial situation.

"Where the fuck are we even at?" I muttered as we climbed in the car and I turned over the ignition.

Nothing. Dead battery, from the sound of it.

"Where the fuck are we?" I asked again, louder this time. I tried to turn the key again. Still nothing. My questions continued,

"Well, how did we get here? What time is it? Did we miss D-Day?"

"I am not sure," Boyd answered, "but I do know one thing.... There is only one remedy for a morning like this," and he produced a skinny, sickly looking joint from his pocket and a flask engraved with the initials R.D.

Boyd gave the flask a little shake,

"Hair of the dog?" he asked, cracking open the top.

"Fuck, why not?" I answered, taking a swig as he lit the joint. Jesus, moonshine is rough in the mornings.

"Who is R.D.?" I asked, as I shook my head to clear the cobwebs.

"No idea, but his flask seems to be full of that godawful fucking moonshine, fire water, fucking nectar of the gods," Boyd answered, taking another long pull at the moonshine before offering it to me. I shook my head, wishing I had a coffee and wondering if they had coffee pots out here in the prostitution district.

We decided right then and there that we shouldn't have gotten carried away on the moonshine with Jimbo. But that's how good moonshine does.

"You think you've got a handle on it, then bam, you're waking up in a dairy barn whorehouse field with no money and a dead battery," Boyd was lamenting our current situation.

"To be fair, we didn't' have any money to begin with," I offered.

"Doesn't change a thing," Boyd countered.

Once we had our minds right, we set about trying to find some jumper cables. As we were searching the trunk, which I knew didn't contain jumper cables, I spied the little redhead dragging a wheeled contraption across the dewy grass. A great big blonde woman was following behind her, trailing a bright orange extension cord behind her.

"Happens all the time!" the little one exclaimed when they reached us.

"Pop the hood and we'll get you set up here," she said with a smile.

They plugged in their jump starter, hooked the cables to the battery, gave it the juice, and we were ready for action. Boyd was sweet talking some directions out of the big blonde while I helped the redhead bring the battery charger and extension cord back into the barn.

"Thanks for your help," I said. "Sorry we can't stay but we have some stuff to take care of."

"I know, I know, you wouldn't shut up about it all night," she said. "Gotta move the body, gotta move the body, so the Mexicans can find it. I never heard anybody so worried about Mexicans finding a body. Ain't they got plenty of them down there? Now they're gonna steal that job too?"

I didn't take the bait and fall into an immigration reform discussion, instead bowing, kissing her on the hand, and saying,

"And now I must be off, my lady, but I hope soon to see you and your lovely countenance once again!" which she smiled at, although she didn't really get it.

"My what?" she asked as I high stepped it out of there, blowing her a kiss over my shoulder. We had lost enough time already.

"So, the directions are pretty easy," Boyd was saying as I got in the car and put it in gear.

"We follow the fence line over to the gate about a half mile, follow that dirt road until it hits blacktop. Make a left on the blacktop and follow it for about four miles until we come to a T intersection. Make a right and we'll be on HWY 63. In Tennessee. Sorta near the interstate I think."

"What?" I said in shock. Tennessee?

"How in the fuck did we end up in Tennessee?"

Boyd's simple answer made all the sense in the world,

"Moonshine."

By the time we made it back to the apartment it was 2 in the afternoon. Luckily, we had not known what time it was until we passed the bank as we got into town. The clock on the radio was off due to the dead battery, and neither of us owned a watch. It was for the best, because we would have been freaking out if we had known how late we were.

We were all the way late.

Twenty-Four

Better Late than Never

By the time we got there, Betty had her distraction BBQ in full swing, and it appeared the whole building was in attendance.

It looked like quite the party. There was a whole spread, burgers, hotdogs, tater salad, chips, coolers of beer and soda, the works. Randy had brought his collection down and was running the music. Saul was posted up near the gas shutoff, picking at some of the potato salad and trying to appear nonchalant.

I looked over to the Lincoln and saw only one-handed Francisco in the car, and no trace of the rest of the crew. Fathead and Big D had their hustle going, and it was working fabulously. Fathead told us all about it, later.

"It was masterful, dog! After I sold them the coke, Big D is fucking around at the pool table and one of them says they want to play and Big D, says he'll play them for the table. Like a game to see who gets to play a game. Not even any money on it, like just for a turn, dog.

"And this motherfucker lays the biggest, baddest hustle on these boys that I have ever seen! Big D nailed the first shot to claim solids, right out of the gate. He never made another shot for at least 15 minutes straight, but he would only leave them with impossible lies, dog! They never had anything to shoot at!

"Big D would miss his shot and leave the ball back behind three of his own balls so they had to keep trying crazy off the wall combos, and jumps and shit, which of course they never hit.

"And all the while, Big D is all like 'o man, tough lie, sorry again fellas.' They even started taking turns trying to make a shot just to get the game moving. He had all four of them fully locked in, and he just kept toying with them. It was awesome, dog!"

Of course, at the time, we didn't know how well it was going. All we knew was we were well behind schedule and we had to hurry.

When we got upstairs to the waiting Room, Fleetwood Mac Laura informed us that Bev and Tweeker Dave had already been gone for an hour and a half. He had brought one jack Russell, but the other was still up there, so she said we would need to be careful.

"No offense, but where did you come from?" I asked Fleetwood Mac Laura.

"Katie invited me, said you two bailed on her," she said simply, as Katie walked by and punched me in the arm, sticking out her tongue at me.

Boyd was standing in the living room with Jesus, looking at the dead Mexican who had been leaned up in the corner of the kitchen. We had tried and tried, but we couldn't think of a good way to get the body upstairs. And now it was too late. The wheels were in motion.

Jesus knew the plan wasn't going right, but like us, he didn't appear to have a clue of how to fix it either. We couldn't just walk the body up there pretending it was Randy, with Randy playing music downstairs in front of Francisco. The Randy outfit, bright orange Vols jacket and hat, were laying over the back of the dinette set chair. I picked them up, hating the fucking Tennessee Volunteers collegiate athletic department even more than usual. Even their apparel seemed to have failed us in the end.

"Useless piece of shit," I snarled as I flung the Randy outfit against the wall. I could hear that little fucking jack Russell up there going ape shit, chasing his own ball, banging into everything it sounded like.

"What the fuck are we- "

I was interrupted by a sudden boom from above us that shook the entire building. Smoke alarms and car alarms started going off all at once, shook up by whatever the fuck had just happened.

"Is that the..." I started to ask, but saw that Boyd had retrieved Hippy John's device from under the sink and was holding it in his hand. Katie and Fleetwood Mac Laura had run outside when we heard the boom, and Katie stuck her head back in the door to yell,

"Tweeker Dave's apartment is on fire! Smoke

and flames pouring out of it! Y'all get out before the roof caves in!"

Boyd, still holding our bomb, started to smile that crazy smile.

"Put Jesus in the Randy suit, quick!" he called as he jumped up on the counter and stuck the bomb on top of the cabinet directly above the dead body.

"Two minutes!" he said excitedly as he hopped down. Jesus had already thrown on the Vols gear, and as all the tenants were rushing in and out of the building, frantically saving their heirlooms and their dope, Jesus walked out the door, down the steps, across the parking lot, and out of our lives.

Francisco and the pool playing henchmen were having a powwow, trying to determine if any of them had seen that Ecuadorian bastard, when the second explosion rocked the building. Hippy John's charge was louder than the first, and it brought down the ceiling/floor between Tweeker Dave's apartment and Hell's Waiting Room.

"Hippy Fucking John," I said in marvel as we watched the smoke pouring out of the Waiting Room.

"The flames seem pretty fitting, don't you think?" Randy asked.

"I mean, I think it's significant. Hell's Waiting Room goes down in flames, freeing all the inhabitants. Don't you get it? We're finally free! And everything that's important is right here," he said, gathering up his cd's and albums.

"I'm going to bring all this over to my dad's so Little Bro can enjoy it when he gets out. And then I'm gonna ask SSGT Jones if I can ship out early. Boyd, Jack, I'm going to miss you guys!"

And Randy scooped us up in a big bear hug, both of us together. Katie got in on it too, tears streaming down her face.

"I'm leaving too," she sobbed. "I wanted to tell you last week but with everything going on..." she trailed off, blew her nose, and continued. "I'm going to Indianapolis with Fleetwood Mac Laura."

"Not if you keep calling me that," Fleetwood Mac Laura chided, as she came up behind Katie and slipped her arms around her. Katie spun around and planted a heavy-duty kiss on her lips.

We all must have been staring, with dumb and surprised looks on our faces, because Katie said,

"Don't look so surprised you bunch off assholes! I can be into chicks, too." And with many a hug and a blown kiss and a 'we'll keep in touch,' Katie rode out of the Waiting Room, having finally found the one to call her name.

"I've known for a while," Randy said proudly as we watched them climbed into Laura's Volkswagen.

"Why do you think it always worked out for us to share a room?" he said.

As the fire department pulled up and started their helter-skelter disembarking procedure, I was about to say something exceedingly clever, when I felt a gun in my back. The chollos had us surrounded as we huddled in the parking lot, and Francisco was in search of answers.

"Where is the Ecuadorian?" he asked. "What is this explosion? What manner of sorcery is this?"

Before we could answer, Tweeker Dave and Bev arrived on the scene. Tweeker Dave did not look as concerned as I had expected him to be. He had a big smile on his face, in fact.

"Yes, yes, yes, this is perfect," he was saying. "Little Charlie must have set off the defensive munitions, poor little feller, but it's all for the best. We aren't covered, nor are we responsible, for acts of God!"

And with that, he picked up the remaining Jack

Russell Terrier and boarded the city bus, never to be seen or heard from again.

"What the hell was that?" Boyd was saying.

Bev answered,

"That crazy motherfucker took me out and didn't even want to do nothin'. All he wanted to do was sit in Starbucks, drink their shitty coffee and tell me about the court case he is building against the government for harassment from where he got a medical waiver for Vietnam and how he kept every medically related receipt and record, even down to the aspirin regimen, having individual daily receipts and records and how he kept track of every band aid he's used for the past 25 years, and he has it all catalogued up there in the apartment in case they come looking for him over the manifesto he sent the government in 1972."

She paused, looked up at the smoke still pouring out of his apartment, and said,

"At least I guess he used to have it all catalogued up there. Said he had it rigged to blow if anybody tried to tamper with it. Guess that other dumbass dog didn't know about the booby traps. I'm still keeping his money though."

And with that she headed off toward her corner, figuring she may as well put in a full day if she'd gone to the trouble of getting all dolled up.

Francisco was shaking his head, trying to process the information he had just heard. I wished we'd had a translator because I felt her testimony had basically exonerated us. But Francisco still needed convincing, especially since his men were becoming more and more agitated. They knew they needed to either kill us or get the hell out of there before the cops really got command of the situation.

Lucky for them, it was the Middlesboro PD, and they weren't used to explosions. Several of the cops were snapping selfies instead of securing the crime scene, so I suggested Francisco and I go check things out in the apartment. I assured him Jesus had not come out with us.

I told him, as we climbed the stairs, that Jesus seemed to have undergone a religious experience over the past couple of days, and that I thought he had wanted to die, probably why he didn't run out when we did.

"But who knows what an Ecuadorian thinks?" I finished as we came to the doorway. Francisco grunted his agreement, himself not really knowing what an Ecuadorian would think about anything.

We walked through the thick smoke as firemen rushed to and fro, telling us we weren't supposed to be there, yet not making us leave either. Hippy John's device had worked perfectly, just enough boom to cave in the ceiling, but the firemen had the flames out already and there was actually very little damage to the rest of the unit.

Besides smoke damage of course. And chunks of dead Mexican out in the living room, just like Hippy John had promised.

Francisco looked at the pieces of carnage that he thought he had been chasing for months. He kicked at an arm, still cloaked in the sleeve of the maintenance jacket. He seemed to have a feeling of peace come over him, and even sort of smiled when he asked if we still had his hand.

I pointed to the freezer, which had some ceiling tile on it, and a dented door.

"Thank you, Gringo," he said as he opened the freezer and grabbed his frozen hand.

"This has been the most difficult case I have worked on. Demons, devils, fires and explosions. And I think my men have succumbed to temptation and bought a large sum of cocaine. But now the quarry is dead, the mission is over. I can return from this stinking fucking country. Finally. Adios!"

And with that, he and his men were gone.

I found Boyd sitting on the dumpster, watching the fire crew mill about, trying to determine the cause of the explosion. They all said how lucky it was that Saul happened to be sitting right down there at the BBQ, next to the gas shutoff. Probably saved all our lives they figured.

"Yep, good thing." I said as I jumped up onto the dumpster top with him. "You think they'll find anything to charge us with up there?"

"I don't believe they will. I don't think the Waiting Room worked that way," he said, a sad faraway look in his eye. "I'm gonna miss that place."

"It didn't look like the damage was that bad..." I started to say, but Boyd cut me off.

"No, man. Randy is right. We've been set free. And I know me and you never felt trapped by it the way some others did. But we both know we had roles to play in there, duties to perform. We were the curators, and now we've been let go from our position."

I had always figured Boyd was the actual curator and I was more of a janitor, but I figured a little posthumous job promotion wouldn't hurt anything.

"So, what do we do now?" I asked. "Follow Tweeker Dave's lead and hop the city bus for a new adventure?"

Boyd smiled, and lit a joint. The cops and firemen were too busy to pay any attention to two dopeheads smoking dope.

"No sir, I think we need something bigger. Greyhound perhaps? Don't you have a friend down in New Orleans we should visit?" he asked, the beginnings of a plan starting to turn the wheels of his mind.

I laughed, and took the joint as he offered to me.

"Absolutely," I said, "the show must inevitably go on."

We hit the road heading south, until we ended up in a waiting room of sorts, commonly called a holding cell. We were in the Big Easy, awaiting arraignment, no bail money and no lawyer.

But we weren't worried.

That waiting room didn't have shit on Hell's Waiting Room.

A naturalized citizen of the South, Mr. Stevens now makes his home in New England writing scathing reviews of local politics,  sea hags, and the wretches of High Society.